THE DRUMMER BOY

THE DRUMMER BOY

LARRY WEINBERG

AN AVON CAMELOT BOOK

THE DRUMMER BOY is an original publication of Avon Books. This work has never before appeared in book form.

AVON BOOKS
A division of
The Hearst Corporation
1350 Avenue of the Americas
New York, New York 10019

Copyright © 1996 by Larry Weinberg
Published by arrangement with the author
Library of Congress Catalog Card Number: 96-96407
ISBN: 0-380-78344-4
RL: 4.9

First Avon Camelot Printing: December 1996

CAMELOT TRADEMARK REG. U.S. PAT. OFF. AND IN OTHER COUNTRIES, MARCA REGISTRADA, HECHO EN U.S.A.

Printed in the U.S.A.

OPM   10 9 8 7 6 5 4 3 2 1

1

The *Indian Maiden* drifted through fog. They had taken down her two sails because Caleb's father thought it too dangerous to be moving toward a rocky coast they could not see. From the sound of breaking ocean waves, they were very near the shore. Back at the tiller, Mr. Peasley stared hard into the haze with smarting eyes. If only he could catch one flicker of the lighthouse warning lamp off Broken Ship's Point, he'd know how to guide the craft into the bay.

But for now, their safety depended on the sharp ears of the boy crouching over the bow with a ten-foot push-off pole in his hands. Like an easily startled seabird, he listened for a special noise—a bubbling splash in between waves, which was the sign of a big rock ahead, just under the surface of the water. The jagged edges of these "sinkers" could gash the bottom out of a boat in no time. But it was a very different noise that Caleb suddenly heard. A cracking boom, something almost like thunder, came from somewhere behind them.

"Haul up the sails!" cried his father, pulling hard on the tiller. "If that's an iceberg breaking up, we'll have a wave that'll lift us right up and throw us into the rocks before we ever get to the bay.''

How many minutes did they have to get far enough out to sea? Since sound carried a good distance over the water, there was no way of telling when the monster wave would roar down on them. What little wind there was came from the wrong direction. But Caleb's father, an even better sailor than a fisherman, maneuvered the sails to catch every stray breath of air. The boat tacked and made some miles of headway. Time passed . . . and still there was no crashing mountain of water.

Mr. Peasley stroked his whiskers. ''Seems to me I was wrong,'' he said. ''But long as we're out here, we'll lower the sails again and wait until this fog lifts. Wouldn't make it back in time to unload our catch at the dealer's wharf anyway. Wonder what that noise was?''

To Caleb, it had sounded like the cannons that boomed good-bye just before his brother Jonathan's regiment went off by train to put down ''the Rebellion.'' He held back from saying it now to avoid another sermon about ''boys who are dying to get into a war where boys are dying.'' Besides, this part of Maine was too far north for any fighting to be going on at sea.

They sat in silence, as they usually did, and his mind began to wander to his favorite daydream of leading a cavalry charge with a saber in his hands.

''I should have listened to your grandfather,'' Mr. Peasley muttered at last. ''He saw a mist over the hills yesterday morning and said to stay in close to shore today because it was going to fog over. I told him April was too early in the year for anything like this.''

''Well, Pa, he's often wrong.''

Amos Peasley let out a sigh. ''No, we just don't listen

2

to him as much now that he's taken to rambling. Besides, I didn't like his saying it when your mother could hear. I didn't need her begging me not to go out with you to where the mackerel were running.''

Suddenly the boy held up his hand. Something had knocked against the boat, moved away, and knocked again. Leaning over, Caleb fished around until his hand touched wood.

''What is it?''

''A box, Pa.'' He pulled it into the boat, found the latch with his fingers, and opened it. ''Empty, though.''

Taking it from his son, Mr. Peasley ran his leathery fingertips over the carved lid. ''From China, I believe,'' he said. ''Your grandfather kept one like it for his private letters and such when he sailed.''

Caleb took a deep breath. ''Pa, that booming before sounded to me a lot like cannon going off.''

Mr. Peasley was silent a few moments. ''Do you hear anything?''

The boy concentrated. ''Coughing. Somebody's coughing.''

''I'm thinking you might hand me my shotgun, son. And then I'd like you to lie down on the deck.''

''No, Pa,'' protested the boy as he gave him the gun. ''I'd have my face in fish.''

''Do what I say.''

Lying there, Caleb recognized other sounds—the sharp creak of oars turning in locks. ''I think it's two boats,'' he whispered to his father. ''Can't tell how far away, though. This fog's throwing me off.''

Hesitating a moment, Mr. Peasley cupped a hand to his mouth, ''Ahoy there! Boat ahead of you. I think you're coming right at us.''

3

"Ahoy, the boat!" a voice trailed back. "This be the captain and crew of the schooner *Yankee Breezes* out of Boston, which was sunk this day by Confederate raiders—blast them! They scuttled my ship and set us off in these dories."

Mr. Peasley lowered the gun. "Anyone hurt?"

"No. That much I can be thankful for. Do ye know where we are?"

"Can't say. Been drifting."

"What are you then and from where?"

"Fishing sloop out of Sunday Cove, north of Bath."

"Sunday Cove? Wait a bit. I know a man from there. He sailed with me around the Horn to China in eighteen hundred and what was it? . . . forty two. Peasley's his name, Artemis Peasley."

"He's talking about Grandpa," Caleb said excitedly.

"Your grandfather do ye say?" called the captain.

"Yes, sir."

"Raise your voice, if you please, lad. Helps us to find you."

"Yes, sir!"

"He's alive, then, I hope?"

"He is, sir. In pretty good shape, too."

"Good. Good. And you and your father have turned fisherman, I take it? You don't go roving this old world like he did? . . . I didn't hear you. Did you say something, lad?"

"No, sir. We just fish."

"Well, don't say it that way, lad. God wants us all to do *something*. My own offspring doesn't even go out on the water for any reason. Want to hear what he told me?"

"Yes, sir."

"He said, 'The sea is a dead place for me, Papa, now

4

that steamers are coming in.' And he said I should retire. But I wouldn't do it while there was a boat with a mast load of sails on her, even if it means going up and down the coast like a peddler, which is what I've become.'' He let out a mournful sigh. ''Well, that's finished now. Insurance company won't pay off for an act of war.''

''What were you carrying?'' called Caleb's father. ''Munitions?''

''Munitions!'' exploded the captain. ''Not unless they've started doing battle with marbles and slingshots, peashooters, clay bubble pipes, cherry-wood cradles, rattles, and bolts of cotton for ladies dresses. Besides which, we were headed north for Nova Scotia, not south for the armies. . . . Do I sound any closer to you?''

''You do. Very close now.''

''Anyway, they put a cannonball across our bow, so we dipped our sails gentle as you please, wanting no trouble and seeing no reason for it. They came on board armed to the teeth like buccaneers, and we showed them what we were carrying. 'The only thing ye can use,' I told them, 'is the federal money in my strongbox and precious little there is of that, but take it.' What long faces they pulled. Oh, but those Johnny Rebs were the disappointedest pirates ever you see.''

As the first of the two dories came dimly into view, Mr. Peasley said, ''They didn't take your ship for a prize?''

''No! What were they going to do with an old two-master that's closer to the grave than I am? Lug it all the way back through the Union blockade to Virginia? If they were men with any decency or sense in 'em, they would have left us alone after that, but they chased us off without any provisions and sent my ship to the bottom. . . . Ahoy, behind me! Are you men following closely? I don't want you wandering now.''

"We're all right, skipper. Coming right along.''

"See you do. Now, what was I saying? Mr. Peasley, I tell you, this destruction had nothing to do with the war. It was just pure meanness! And old as I am . . . and with as little as I've cared to have anything to do with this or any other war, I'm going to find a way to pay them back! That is the promise of Benjamin T. Boggs.''

"I have heard your name, sir, on my father's lips,'' said Mr. Peasley, dropping anchor just before the lead boat pulled alongside and shipped oars. The fog was so thick that no one's face could be made out clearly. Leaning over the side, Caleb's father reached out to find and shake hands with a thick-bearded old man. "But I'm afraid there's nothing to offer you and your crew unless they like raw mackerel with the scales still on.''

"I daresay I've dined on worse than that in my time,'' said Boggs, turning now to shake Caleb's hand as well. "Heave us in a few, just in case we have trouble making it to the shore for a while. And do you have any water to spare?''

Caleb, who stood closer to the barrel, waited to hear what his father would say. "We've a quarter of a cask, and you're welcome to most of it.''

Caleb tipped some water into a bottle, corked it, put it away, and handed over the cask to the man sitting at the nearest oar. Besides himself and the captain there were four others. The cask was passed round from mouth to mouth, then was handed back to Caleb. He gave it to a man in the second rowboat, which had just come alongside.

"Thank you kindly,'' said the fellow. "Where I come

6

from, the feller you help out always tells you his name. That way you can run into him some year and remind him, if need be, to return the favor. The name's Joshua Gooden, and I was the first mate.''

"I'm Caleb. Pleased to meet you, Mr. Gooden.''

"Likewise. How old are you, Caleb?''

"Fourteen . . . going on.''

"Big for your age, I see. You must be pretty strong from hauling in those long fishing lines and tugging on lobster traps.''

"Enough, I guess,'' Caleb said, without showing any pride in his voice, though he was beginning to feel it.

"Wishing you was off to the navy so you could go and fight, I'll bet.''

Caleb glanced at his father, who was talking to the captain. He lowered his voice. "Yes, sir, I surely do.''

"Twisted up my leg in a fall off a crow's nest or I'd be in the service myself. Any kinfolk in the war?''

"My brother, but he went down into the army.''

The first mate, waiting till last to take his drink, handed back the cask. "That's suprisin' from a seagoing family,'' he said, wiping his mouth on his arm. "Fighting on the sea is a cleaner life. And a more fitting death, too, if you have to have one.''

Caleb thought he was probably right, but he didn't want to talk about it anymore. There hadn't been any word from his brother since early December, when many a lad from Maine had been killed storming the hills at the great battle of Fredericksburg, nearly a thousand miles away in Virginia. The long days and nights of waiting since then had put a tremble into the corners of his mother's firm mouth and was streaking her long dark hair with gray. Her almost daily letters to the War Office in

Washington seemed to disappear into a bottomless black hole, because no answer ever came back.

And this morning while it was still dark, Caleb descended from his room to find his mother asleep at the writing desk, pen fallen from her hand and the whale-oil lamp still flickering. The letter she'd been writing began, ''Dear President Lincoln, I write to you as a mother in despair . . .''

Caleb's eyes began to grow hot, and out of respect for her privacy he didn't read the rest of it. He just covered her shoulders with her shawl and went out the back parlor door through the yard to the icehouse.

But would his mother have worried just as much about him, he couldn't help asking himself as he filled up buckets with shelled clams for bait. ''Well, of course she would!'' he told himself. He repeated it again for good measure while he carried the buckets down the slope to the pier where the *Indian Maiden* was tied. Still and all, that question kept coming up lately. He had always known that Jonathan was special in his mother's heart, being the first of three babies she hadn't lost in childbirth. But that had nothing to do with loving both her sons the same, did it?

''Well, look there. Fog's lifting!'' declared Captain Boggs, jarring Caleb back to the present.

Curling upwards like cigar smoke, the mist lifted slowly from the surface of the water and dissolved altogether. The first stars of an evening sky appeared. Off to the left, where the dark outline of the Maine coast rose in the distance, the men could see the last rays of sunset. Caleb's father pointed northwest to the circling gleam of the lighthouse at Broken Ship's Point near the mouth of the bay. Now father and son knew where they were. They hadn't drifted far at all.

The men in the dories, too, began to grow cheerful. "By the Great Horn Spoon," said the old man, "now we don't have to eat raw mackerel after all."

Caleb held up the carved box. "Sir, could this be yours?"

"Why, I believe it is. But you keep it, young fellow. Put it in your seabag the first day you ship out to seek your fortune."

The Peasleys exchanged looks, and Caleb's father said, "You're all welcome to come home to our dinner table, Captain Boggs. I'm sure my father will be joyful to see you. Then you'll stay with us, and we can put down bedding in the church for your crew."

"Most kind, most kind," said the captain enthusiastically.

"Run up the sails, son," Mr. Peasley said, starting to haul anchor while the oarsmen in the two other boats rowed for shore.

Caleb whispered in his father's ear, "But what will Mama say, all of them coming without any warning?"

"Take her mind off her troubles for a while," his father whispered back. "And save me from the tongue lashing she'll give me because of you."

"Me! What for?"

"You ask me that? Why, because I took you this far out of the bay when your grandpa predicted there'd be fog. You don't know yet that you're more precious to her than any day's load of mackerel?"

Caleb swallowed hard. The notion of his mother being worried about him made him happy. To hide his embarrassment, he said, "But we weren't in no real danger, Pa."

9

"Weren't in any real danger," corrected his father. "I won't have her saying I'm letting your grammar go to ruin now you've given up school to take your brother's place . . . for a while."

The *Indian Maiden* made better time into the bay than the dories as they rowed toward the village waterfront. As Mr. Peasley suspected, it was too late to unload the day's catch at the fish dealer's wharf. But the town crier was standing there with his big bell in hand. He knew that one of the boats was very late in returning and was waiting for news.

As soon as the crier saw them, he turned away, clanging his bell and began calling, "Here ye! Here ye! Last boat is in from the fog, and all's well!"

"Mr. Culpepper!" shouted Caleb's father to get his attention. "Got more news for you. We've got a dead ship's crew coming in on dories, and I'm putting them up at the church. No one injured, but can you get the telegraph operator to go back to his office? There's a Confederate raider prowling out there somewhere!"

Docking the boat at its little landing, they set up the rocky slope to the house. You couldn't tell from all the fresh smelling white paint covering its two stories and attic that it's timbers had been waging a war with the salt air for over a hundred years. As father and son kicked off their boots and entered through the kitchen door they sniffed tobacco—and something more than that, the sharp smell of wool being singed and about to burn. Grandpa Peasley, as always, was leaning back in his rocker, with his stockinged feet propped up so close to the cookstove that they were almost in the wood fire.

Shoving his corncob pipe to one corner of his mouth, he exclaimed out of the other corner. "Ye see, Dora? Ye see? You was feared all this time for nothing. Absolutely nothing. I tell ye, the life of a fisherman's wife is a snap. Why it ain't no circumstance at all compared to a sailing man's. Your family comes home every night of the week and doesn't leave it on a Sabbath. But the mother of my own children, may she rest in peace, saw me no more than fifty or sixty days out of a year, if that. Even so, she was ready by the end of my stay to have me out of her hair so she could run her own house proper without me clomping about, making a mess of it."

Mildred Peasley turned around from the table and without a word went to the big simmering kettle of fish stew.

"I'm sorry, old dear. I should have known better than taking Caleb so far out there today," said her husband softly, and waited for a reply. When he got none, he asked in a choked voice, "Nothing in the mail today?"

She shook her head.

"Not a letter," declared Grandpa, swinging around in his rocker and scooting it across the room. "But neither was there any telegram, and every day without one o' them is a blessing, as far as I'm concerned. It's the telegram that brings the bad news. So why don't we all stop worrying for one day more about what we can't change anyways?"

"The train that comes up from Washington will be in Bath tomorrow," Mrs. Peasley said with sudden passion. "And I want Caleb to meet it. There might be some soldiers coming back who can tell us about Jonathan." Though the room was toasty, she pulled her shawl more closely around her.

"But Mildred, the boy's gone down there every Saturday for the last five. Nobody could tell us anything. And now—''

Caleb saw the edges of his mother's mouth begin to twitch. "I'll go anyway, Papa."

"And now, Dora, the mackerel are really running."

"What do I care about mackerel!" Mrs. Peasley snapped.

"But life goes on, don't you see? It has to. That's the only way."

"Life!"

Caleb jumped in. "Papa, let me go."

"Yes, let him," wheezed the old man. "And tomorrow I'll go put out the lines with ye myself."

"No, Cap'n, you're staying here in your rocker," Amos Peasley said, then paused a moment. "Dora, I'm being selfish. Please forgive me. Of course he can go. He'll take the buggy."

"Thank you," she murmured, reaching out for her husband's hand without looking at him. "But Caleb won't need it. Abigail will be going with him. She told me today she wanted to, and she'll be here come daylight in her father's rig. Now everyone wash up and sit down at the table."

Caleb gave his father a meaningful look, which old sharp-eyed Cap'n Peasley caught. He sat forward in his chair. Something was in the air, and he loved anything new that could bring some excitement back into his existence.

"We've got company, I'm afraid, Dora. We came across twelve men in the fog whose ship went down. They're just docking and coming up behind us. We came across them lost in the fog. And I couldn't not invite them. There's many a seafaring man in this family has had to count on strangers when trouble came.''

Caleb's mother stood in silence before the stove. Finally she shrugged. ''You needn't have made a speech about it, Amos. I am a minister's daughter, and I have some sense about what's right and proper. Of course they're very welcome. There's plenty in the kettle, and I'll make more. I'll need Caleb to help me by setting up the front parlor, if that's all right now that he's a man.''

The boy sprang through the kitchen at once. ''Sure, Mama, I'll be glad to. And Grandpa,'' he called back brightly, ''there's a big surprise for you, name of Captain Boggs!''

''Boggs!'' The old man fairly leaped out of his chair and ran to the door. ''Ye old belaying pin!'' he cried. ''What do ye mean by losin' a whole ship?''

''At least I still had one!'' came the returning cry.

''Come in here before you drop your rudder and can't steer your way into the house!''

2

Caleb's mother had no need to start cooking anything else. Soon after the castaways arrived, her kitchen was stormed by other wives carrying fruits, buckets of chowder, trays of cakes, even bunches of springtime flowers. They wouldn't hear of the men going to sleep on the narrow benches of the church and dragged them off to different homes. Often as not the sailors slept in beds left empty by sons who'd gone off to war.

Late into the night Caleb sat at the feet of the two sea captains, feeding logs into the cookstove while he listened to their stories. They talked of bursting island volcanoes and painted cannibals in war canoes, of hunting whales and fighting sharks, and of standing among gigantic statues of strange gods.

This was one time when Grandpa's mind was keen and his memory even keener. He remembered the rescuing of a crew whose ship had struck a reef and was sinking. When he ordered ropes to be thrown across to the other ship's sloping deck, the crew swarmed on board to safety. But their captain began acting strangely and seemed very anxious for Peasley to sail away with them at once.

"I couldn't understand a thing like that, a skipper not wanting to stand by and say farewell to his ship in her dying moments. But then I heard wails and screams. *Human* screams. She was a slaver, don't you know, carrying 'black ivory'—though it was already against the law. I realized he was going to let 'em all sink to the bottom of Davy Jones's locker rather than let on what he'd been up to. Well, I jumped over and went down into the hold where the water was pouring in. One hundred fifty-two souls in chains, they were! My own lads and I had a time of it getting them out—but it wasn't possible to take them all the way back to Africa, sorry to say. Had to find an island with fresh drinking water, some fruit trees, and a good chance for spearfishing."

Sadly, Caleb's grandfather added, "Best I could do." He pulled at his pipe. "Should have put that criminal and his men off on the same island an' let justice be done. Lord, how I despise the trading in slaves!"

"I'm glad to see that Mr. Lincoln finally made up his mind to free the ones we've already got over here," declared Captain Boggs.

"Me, too," agreed Grandpa. "Otherwise, I really don't see what this terrible war is for."

"Why, to save the United States of America from being broken in two parts!" blurted Caleb. "That's why Jonathan went."

Grandpa seemed bewildered for a moment, then his jaw set. "No he didn't!" the old man cried. "Jonathan went because his blood was fired up even though he was fixing to get married. The rest of it was an *excuse*." The old man leaned over the side of his chair and jabbed the stem of his pipe at the boy. "And *you're* just hoping all this craziness will last long enough for you to find the same excuses for yourself! Only no one here is going to buy that same bill of goods twice!''

Caleb felt his face go hot, but Captain Boggs came to the rescue. ''Don't mock him, Artemis. He's no different from young men the world over. Full of beliefs and hot for medals. I heard tell you were a wild one yourself in 1812. All fired up against the British and ready to take on their whole fleet singlehanded.''

''Yes, I was,'' Grandpa admitted grumpily, ''and foolish, too. But we all go to our maker soon enough, and I don't want any of my grandchildren beating me to it.'' Shoving the pipe back into his mouth, he tried to take a draw on it. There was only the gurgling sound of his own saliva.

As a peacemaking gesture, Caleb jumped to his feet. ''It's been out awhile, Grandpa, you just didn't notice it. Let me fill it up for you.''

''Do I look to you, boy, like I can't do for myself?''

''No.''

''Then why ain't you in bed already when tomorrow's a fishing day?''

''Not going fishing tomorrow, Gramps. Going down to Bath with Abby to see if we can find out anything about Jonathan.''

''Abby?'' A blank look crossed his grandfather's face. ''Who's Abby?''

''Why, Abigail Ames. You met her a hundred times, Gramps. She's that schoolteacher from Wiscasset who Jonathan's going to marry. Don't tell me you can't remember her?''

''Not just that moment, I didn't.'' The old man pushed to his feet, sputtering with anger. ''But I'd like to know what gives a pup like you the right to correct me like

16

that in front of my friend, so he can go away from here thinking there's something missing from my mind!''

"Grandpa, I'm sorry. I'm real sorry.''

"Say your goodnights then and go to bed." He sank back into his rocker.

"Goodnight, sir. Goodnight, Captain Boggs.''

Walking out, Caleb heard Boggs say, " 'Tain't the boy's fault you can't hold on to the newer memories, Artemis. It's your own doing.''

"Now ain't that the dumbest thing ever I heard? How's it my fault? I'm eighty-three years of age.''

"Being *old* with the seat of your pants stitched into a chair in your daughter-in-law's kitchen is a lot different from being old standing up in a gale on the bridge of a deck. What kind of memories do you make for yourself shipwrecked here?''

"By thunder, you are right! Let's you and me find us a berth in the navy somewheres and go sink Confederate raiders!''

"That's the ticket,'' chuckled Boggs. "And I'll sign on under you.''

It seemed to Caleb that he had barely set his head down on the pillow when a clang of pans awakened him. He went to the stairs, yawning and stuffing his shirttail back into his trousers. Abby was already in the house, saying to his mother, "If Caleb can leave right away, there's no fear that growing boy of yours will starve without breakfast. There's so much food in the two baskets I packed last night, he'll be eating all day long. Besides, if some bridge is out along the way, we'll lose time going roundabout. I just want to make sure we're at the station before the train comes in.''

17

Caleb's mother lifted an eyebrow as he came down. "Your hairs are standing like celery stalks, young man. Brush them down and get going."

Running fingers through his locks, he turned towards the front door.

"I said *brush*."

"That's all right," said Abby, winking at Mrs. Peasley, "I never look at him anyway."

A grunted little "Umm" rose to his mother's lips. It was as close to a chuckle as she could manage. "Very wise. But will you make sure he's presentable when those soldiers get off the train? I don't want them thinking a lieutenant's brother is an ignorant ragamuffin."

"No son of yours could be ignorant," Abby said fondly, "no matter *how* hard he tries to be. But if you want to give me his textbooks quickly, we can do his Latin and Greek on the way down, algebra and grammar on the way back."

Caleb shot her his darkest look. She merely grinned at him. "You seem very lighthearted today, Abby," Mrs. Peasley said, searching her future daughter-in-law's face.

"Well, that's true," said Abby, although her face clouded over for the briefest moment. "If you won't think of me as superstitious, I'll tell you why. Jonathan came to me in a dream last night. He held up his arm to show me where he pinned my locket and said he was all right."

Caleb's mother gripped Abby's arm. "Bless you, child, for trying to keep my spirits up! I only wish I'd allowed the two of you to marry before he went. You could have been carrying his baby and my grandchild by now."

"It will happen . . . *Mother* . . . . It will. I know it."

The two woman embraced. Grandpa, who'd overheard,

came out of the kitchen, pulling his rocking chair under him. "The main thing to remember is that the Peasley men keep their wits about them in any kind of danger. It's what comes from living a life in touch with the sea. So if anybody's made it out of that battle alive—"

Though intended to be helpful, the old man's words only upset Mrs. Peasley more. "Yes, but all the families except ours have had news already about their sons! One way or the other, they've *heard!*"

"But . . . but maybe Jonathan was on a secret mission!" cried Caleb suddenly. "I bet he'd be the first one they'd send to find out what the enemy was planning. Don't forget he's been down south before in Charleston and New Orleans and—"

Mrs. Peasley swung around to call out to her husband in the kitchen. "Amos? Did you hear what he said?"

"I heard," Caleb's father sighed. "Well, it's something to think about, I suppose."

Abby pressed the boy's shoulder, murmuring, "Go." They went out quickly to her open carriage and didn't speak again until it had rattled past the house. "After this," she said, letting the reins settle in her lap, "I won't be making any more trips down to the railroad."

Her grim remark went though Caleb like a knife. It was almost as if she believed his brother was dead! "But your *dream* and what you said . . . ?"

"We all make things up for your mother, including you, Caleb."

He swiveled in his seat. "Don't you love Jonathan anymore?"

"That's so unfair to suggest!"

He felt terrible. "Look, we can't give up."

"We have to do it *sometime,* Caleb. That's the way

19

we . . ." Shakily she broke off, and started again. "That . . . that's how we first start to mend. . . ."

Caleb saw her bite her lip. He knew she was unhappy, yet he could not go easy on her, not while she was getting ready to bury his brother in her mind. "So then, why," he demanded, "are we going down to the station now?"

"I'm not even sure anymore. I imagine it's just so your mother will feel that *something* is being done. But if I'm going to do anything, Caleb, I want it to be *real*. If my town can find someone to replace me at the end of this term, I'm going to see about becoming a war nurse. They are taking women into the hospitals now, even if the army doesn't like it."

He slid down in his seat, staring glumly into the woods at the side of the road. Soon they left the bay behind and turned off the narrow shore road onto the highway that led down to the city of Bath.

It was a long ride, and from time to time Caleb asked to take his turn at the reins. Abby shook her head, saying the driving relaxed her. Once or twice, though, he thought he heard a sob and glanced at her. But her head was always slightly turned away. Giving up, he let his mind wander. It was easy enough after so little sleep to nod off and drift into dreams.

The joggling of wooden planks beneath the horse's hoofs caused his eyes to open. They were on the paddle-wheel ferry, casting off to cross the Kennebec River, with its great shipyards and docks on the other side. He glanced up at the sky. The sun was already slanting a few degrees to the right of due south. By his reckoning, it was a few minutes after two in the afternoon. He checked the brass pocket watch his grandfather had given him for his thirteenth birthday. Two seventeen—not bad figuring. They were early, too, since the train wasn't due until four.

Early, yes, but the open platform of the Portland and Kennebec Railroad was already crowded with people. Among the eager faces of waiting parents he saw children all dressed up in Sunday go-to-church clothes and clutching little American flags. There were social club ladies getting ready to greet each of the returning heroes with wonderful-smelling bundles of lilacs. He saw the town's marching band busily tuning up its big horns.

Except for a lineup of empty homemade wheelchairs, all this activity made Caleb think of happier doings, like parades and fairs. There were even a few food and drink stands. A dime of his own money bought lemonade and doughnuts for Abby and himself. She seemed to have perked up, too, and went back to her old habit of teasing him. "Why, if I were teaching a class on how to become a perfect gentlemen, you would pass with flying colors."

Ribbing he could easily handle, but when she put her hand lightly on his arm, he began to blush. There were times lately when he had certain feelings while he was alone with Abby that were making him uneasy.

As the moment of arrival drew near, everyone on the platform grew more agitated. Adults whispered calming words to each other. The boys started to push each other or pull the girls' braids, or else had to be kept from running too near the tracks. Everyone, meanwhile, kept their ears perked for the sound of an engine. But the minutes went by . . . and then the hours . . . while the only noises in the distance came from the hammers, mallets, saws, and shouts of the nearby shipyards.

The sun had set when the stationmaster announced that the train had been delayed below Boston to make way

21

for troop carriers heading in the other direction. "Sorry, folks," he said, "but it could be a real long wait."

The band stuffed all the horns and drums into a big cart and departed. The ladies of the flower baskets carried their gifts into the stationmaster's office and left them there. Parents put their little ones to sleep in their buggies while deciding whether to stay on or not. Caleb and Abby had been through all this a couple of times before, and they had no intention of leaving. Slowly they finished off the turkey sandwiches she had prepared. Then they walked around a bit. Finally, when the air grew colder, they wrapped themselves with blankets and stretched out on two benches to doze.

The heat of the stationmaster's lantern in his face roused Caleb. Abby was already sitting up, talking to the man. "I'm going off duty, miss, and there's probably no sense to you staying out here in the chill. The train won't be coming in till morning. It's been sidetracked."

"What time in the morning?"

"Can't say. Telegraph's closed down for the night. Is it too far for you to go home and come back?"

"Yes, it is."

"Well, there are some boarding places in town, though it's a bit late to knock on any doors. But there's an all-night eatery down by the shore called the Tars and Spars. It's a decent enough place, miss, if you don't mind some carpenters and ship's crew. They've got army guards patrolling the loading docks just outside of it, and you won't find any drunks or troublemakers in there."

"Thank you kindly," she said. "I, uh, I don't suppose you'd know if there are any men on board from the Twentieth Maine?"

"I expect there are a few from all the state regiments,

22

some who've been let out of the hospitals down in Washington and some whose enlistment is up."

Caleb untied the horse from the post by the watering trough, fed it some carrots from his hand, and hitched it up to the buggy. He drove this time, putting the horse into a slow trot, and in a little while they were entering the crowded, smoke-filled shop. A man holding a steaming mug of coffee stood up and called, "Peasley."

Until the fellow limped a step or two from his table, Caleb didn't recognize Joshua Gooden, the first mate from the sunken trader. Gooden invited them to sit with him, saying, "Your sweet mother stuffed me as full as a goose when I sat down at her table, and I'd be obliged if you'd let me do the same for the both of you. I had heard that you were coming down to Bath, and why. Any news?"

"Not yet. The train's been stalled. I'm really surprised. How did you get here ahead of us?"

"Oh, I didn't stay last night, like the captain. Neither did two of the other men. There was a mail packet came by making up time for the fog and steaming down this way. The lads who came with me are bound for home and family, but I've got me a berth as bosun on the *Dolphin*. That's the one with the three tall masts out there and her running lights on. Even with all her sails still down, isn't she a beauty of a windjammer? Soon as the tide is up, we'll be on our way to pay Johnny Reb back."

Caleb's eyes widened. "Why, where are you going?"

"What will it be, folks?" asked the owner of the shop, coming over in an apron.

Gooden waited until they gave their order, then he leaned forward in a mock whisper. "Supposed to be a military secret, but them soldiers on the dock with fixed

23

bayonets gives it away from the start. She's being fitted on with a couple twelve-pound cannon to fight her way along if she has to. We're bound to Washington with supplies for whichever one of our generals that old devil Robert E. Lee is likely to beat the stuffing out of next. Right now, they're just loading on supplies for the ship. But in New York we'll take on all manner of explosives, so it'll be a little tricky if we run into trouble after that, even with them new guns. Not to mention that a sailor throwing a harpoon might hit something—but whether any of us can do it with a big gun is a question. Still and all, I'm glad to be going to sea again!" He gave Caleb a broad wink. "I'll bet you'd love to be on her yourself, hey?"

The boy noticed Abby's face take on a set like his mother's. "He's a *schoolboy,* Mr Gooden."

"But I'm not one anymore."

"You *will* be when Jonathan gets back. You're only taking his place on the boat for a little while."

"I wouldn't want to butt into family matters," said the seafarer carefully when the boy darted him a pleading look. "But the sea is an education, too, miss. I was twelve when I left home."

"So was my grandfather!"

"Caleb, those were different times. And I'm sure that Mr. Gooden will agree there's a new world starting up. A man will need a formal education to get ahead."

"My sea chest is full of books, miss. I've read all the great ones and *been* most everywhere they talk about."

Abby may have caught herself sounding too much like a stern schoolmarm. "Well, I do suppose there are different roads to learning . . ."

24

Caleb nearly jumped from his seat. "Then maybe you can talk to my ma and pa for me!"

"Here comes the food. Eat your eggs before I throw them at you!"

Well, so much for that. Joshua Gooden gave the boy a warning look, and the subject was quickly changed.

It was shortly before daylight that Caleb and Abby drove back to the station. After all their efforts to meet the train when it came in, they were late. Folks had already picked up their loved ones. Buggies were rolling away, and only a small group of soldiers still remained. They were watching a few coffins draped with American flags being unloaded onto a two-horse hay wagon. Forming a little line beside it, they came to attention and saluted as the wagon rattled slowly past them.

One of the men managed to do this in spite of being on crutches. Another, who was a corporal, used his left hand in place of the right, which was missing. As soon as he lowered it, Abby recognized him.

"Silas!" In an instant she was out of the carriage, running to him. Caleb watched the soldier's hard-lined face open into a smile. He watched her clasp the man's only hand in the two of hers and bring them to her cheek.

Caleb stepped down, but hung back. He didn't know of any close relatives that Abby had in the army. In fact, he was pretty sure she *didn't* have any! So then, what was all *this* about? Who was this fellow anyway? And why was she being so . . . well, whatever that was . . . with anybody else but Caleb's brother? He watched her touch the empty sleeve of the man's blue jacket. Now he was touching *her* arm! He seemed to be comforting her.

"Actually, I've been pretty lucky," Caleb heard him gently say. "All those arms and legs that were sawed off in that field hospital, and there were only four of us I know of who didn't die from the shock of it.''

"Is there anyone coming to take you back to Wiscasset?" she asked, wiping the corners of her eyes. "If not, I have room for you and at least one other."

"Thanks, Abby, I'll take you up on it. The others'll wait, I think. No, I didn't write ahead to my folks. Someone else would have had to do it for me, and I just didn't care for that. Have to train myself to scribble with my left. Say, maybe you'll even help me with it, if that's all right, being a schoolteacher and all?"

As they turned toward the carriage the one-armed corporal took notice of Caleb standing beside it. He was about to nod to the boy when Abby said, "That's Jonathan Peasley's brother."

The man stopped suddenly. The others turned quickly to stare. Abby grew anxious. "Oh, Silas, can you tell me what's happened to him? There've been no letters since just before Fredericksburg and no telegrams about him either. His mother writes constantly to the War Department but doesn't get any answers. Caleb and I have been down here five times to speak to other men coming back, but either they weren't in the same regiment or they were in a different company. But you were in G Company, weren't you? I mean, everyone from Sunday Cove and from Wiscasset were together, isn't that so?"

Silas had dropped his eyes to his feet. "Well, yes and no. Things got shuffled about after a while, what with one thing and another . . ." He fidgeted uneasily.

"You do know something. I can see it."

"I . . . uh . . . I'm just not the one to talk about it, Abby. Not after all the years we've know each other."

Abby wrung her hands, darting looks from one man to another.

"Go ahead, Corporal," called the soldier on crutches. "She'll have to find out sometime."

But he remained silent.

"Why are you holding back from me? Silas, for God's sake, *talk!*"

Caleb had had enough of this. "What is it?" he called. "Is my brother dead?"

Nobody answered, but one of the men turned his head away. Caleb was almost sure he saw the fellow spit on the ground.

Abby touched Silas's good arm. "Was he wounded?" Slowly he shook his head.

"Then my brother's missing in action, is that it?"

All the men were staring at him again, studying him up and down. "Now that I take a good look, he's just like him," one of them muttered.

"That doesn't mean we have to take it out on the boy!" Silas snapped.

"Take *what* out on me?" Caleb croaked though a throat so tight he could hardly get the words out.

"Jonathan betrayed us on that hill," Silas shot out. "Now I admit that we were all shaking in our . . ."

"What did you say about my brother?" the boy screamed.

"Caleb, hear him out!"

"What! You're going to listen to this?"

"I don't have to believe it. I just have to hear!"

"We were all shaking in our boots," he went on. "It was the worst mistake the army ever made to order that attack. Well, at least the Twentieth Maine didn't go in the first day of the fighting. The other regiments were

27

already blown to pieces when they sent us up. When the enemy began to tear us apart with cross fire, we dove face down on the field, using the bodies around us for shields. We were pinned down there for hours when Colonel Chamberlain told us we had a special job to do. He had us crawl up the rest of that slope. We got so close to the stone fence at the top that we could hear the Rebs talking to each other. Meanwhile, we were being left by ourselves. The rest of the army was sneaking back over the river where our own big guns could finally cover them. Think of it, Abby—just a few hundred of us were supposed to trick the whole Confederate army, about thirty thousand men, out of charging down the hill before everyone else could get away. Suddenly your Lieutenant Peasley got to his feet and began screaming, 'For God's sake, Colonel, get ourselves out of here! Our whole army is back across the river!' ''

''My brother never said that!'' Caleb barked.

''Then how come I heard it, too?'' said another wounded soldier. ''The rebs would have charged down on us right then if it wasn't for the Colonel thinking fast and bellowing back, 'Men, arrest that *lying* traitor and hold fast! This is a trick of the enemy to get us all to stampede.' Well, Abby, it worked, because the rebels didn't come storming down after us. But even so, we took a lot of fire because of that. On our way down from there, that's when I was hit. Others, too.''

By now, an angry fire was raging so out of control inside of Caleb that it wrenched his whole body. He wanted to throw himself at this man and everyone who agreed with him! But how do you attack wounded people? What he had to do was stop this lie and keep it from being repeated to others!

"Now you see here!" the boy shouted. "It was night, wasn't it? It was dark, wasn't it? That's how you were able to get so close to the enemy, yes or no?"

There was a silence. "All right, yes," said one of the men. "Go on."

"So then . . ." Caleb was suddenly out of breath and sputtering. "So . . . so then, how can you be so sure it really was my brother and not somebody else?"

On the faces around him, Caleb began to see looks of pity. That . . . that was the worst of all!

"Look, I know how hard this is . . ." the corporal began slowly.

"Never mind that!" Caleb boomed. "Just answer my question!"

"Well, I'll give you that I didn't see his face when he ran past me to get away from there. I was belly down on the ground. But I saw that locket he always pinned on his sleeve so he could look at her picture just before we went into action." His gaze flickered in Abby's direction.

Her voice was so weak that Caleb could hardly hear it. "You say he ran away?"

"Never showed up at the river with the rest of us," one of the men said.

There was silence, and a third soldier added, "We heard later on that some of the deserters hid out in the daytimes and got all the way to the West Virginia mountains where they could find other clothes and lose themselves. Learned that back in Washington, but we don't know of any deserters from the Twentieth Maine, though, 'cept him."

This was the same man who Caleb thought might have spat on the ground before. There was no mistaking his doing it now before going on. "Silas don't want to say this to you, but I can. Them deserters has probably found new lives for themselves now. There's plenty of rebel widows in those hills who are willing to hide even a Yankee who can work a farm and help raise their father-less children."

Caleb watched the one-armed corporal touch his broth-er's intended bride for the second time. "I'm sorry, Abby. But if the army ever gets its hands on Jonathan, even Abraham Lincoln wouldn't save him from a firing squad. Some men do break down. But the way he did it . . . and the fix he put us all in . . . Well, the sooner you get over him the—"

"And who's going to help her," the boy suddenly sneered. "You?"

"I didn't say that."

"You're sweet on her. I can see it! You want her to believe this lie!"

"Well, the first part of what you said is true enough." He stared evenly at the boy. "But it's no part of my nature to lie."

Caleb could not bear another second of this. There was nothing he could smash with those fists that kept opening and closing. Not a thing he could do to change what these men would say. And Abby—that look on her face! He whirled away. He ran.

She chased after him, begging him to stop.

He turned his head to scream, "You stay away from me! You believe them!"

"No, I don't! Wait!"

He stopped. But as she came toward him something made him back away, something that was rising up inside of him and taking him over. His ears rang, and he heard his voice over it calling, "*My brother* couldn't do a thing like that—not Jonathan Peasley! And I'll prove it! I'll show you and everyone! Don't you dare believe what they say about my brother!"

He ran toward the docks, not letting himself think another thought. Panting for breath, he flew into the Tar and Salt, looking for Joshua Gooden. But only old ex-sailors were in there now, hunched over their coffee cups and gazing out into the harbor. He whirled round. Through the window, he saw the windjammer moving out, though its sails were still down. A steam tug had hold of it with grappling lines and was pulling it clear of the crowded harbor. Bounding outside, he collided so hard with a patrolling sentry that the fellow went reeling, landed on his backside, and his musket went off.

From different directions, a crowd of running dock workers came rushing to see what had happened. They gathered around the confused soldier, and while he was still trying to collect his wits, Caleb dashed down to the waterfront, ran past a row of beached sailboats until he found a dory with the oars inside, and pushed off into the harbor.

This was stealing, and there was no way of getting around that! Now it would go down in Saint Peter's ledger that Caleb Peasley had broken the Seventh Commandment. Caleb could bear this as far as it came to his own punishment, but what if his sin in some way would stop him from coming to the aid of his brother? He jumped from the boat and shoved it back toward the shore.

Icy water filled his boots so fast that he could barely

pull them out of the sucking mud. Quickly he undid them, then threw off his drenched jacket and began swimming.

It seemed a hopeless thing to do. How would he ever catch up to that ship? Now his trousers were coming down around his legs. With stiffening fingers he pulled them off, too. It was strange how his arm muscles began to burn while he felt so cold. He could hardly feel his feet anymore. But he looked back and his legs were still kicking up water. He didn't dare gaze ahead for fear the ship was getting farther and farther away from him.

Suddenly the tug pulling the ship slowed. The grappling ropes came off the ship. The sails were run up. Caleb would not have noticed this even if he'd been looking. Along with the growing numbness, Caleb was becoming drowsy. It was a merciful sort of forgetfulness. This was nature's way of allowing someone to freeze or drown without going through the fear of dying.

But just as mercifully, a hook on the end of a long pole reeled him in like a fish. Strong hands lifted him from the water. And Caleb tumbled unconscious into the little launch that was carrying the *Dolphin*'s captain out to join his crew.

3

Caleb awoke in a bed screwed down to a floor that was slowly rocking. He was wearing a flannel nightgown that was far too large for him and he lay under a mountain of covers. He was damp from sweating, but when he tried to push the covers away, his arms felt weak. Though he sat up slowly, the movement made him woozy headed. He had to blink hard to clear his eyes before looking through an open porthole at waves. They were rolling away from him toward a distant shoreline. None of these sights fit with what he last remembered. He recalled being in the water, feeling cold, and growing numb. Or had he been imagining things?

So were these new visions part of the same dream? From aloft he heard the sharp flap of canvas sails snapping in the wind. From closer by came the shouting of an order, then a stomping of many feet across wooden boards. No, it felt too real . . .

"I made it!" he cried aloud with the strength that victory brings, and his feet hit the floor.

"Where are my clothes?" Pants and shirt were hanging from a hook, and they were not only dry but felt washed. Dressing quickly, he started to look around for his boots before it came to him how he'd left them behind, and his jacket as well. He stepped barefoot into a little hall that led into the captain's chart room just outside the poop deck, in the stern of the boat. A thin man with mustaches drooping all the way down to his sharp little beard sat at a desk writing in his logbook.

He looked up when the boy entered, "Ah, how the young bounce back like Indian rubber balls. I thought you'd be at least another day or two in sick bay. But now what do I do with you, Caleb Peasley?"

"How do you know who I am?"

"I didn't until the bosun who has charge of men on the first watch came forward to tell me who you were. Well he *was* my petty officer. I had to demote him for giving away the secret of where we were bound and why."

"You punished Joshua because of me?"

"Everything one does in this world has a consequence, young man, for good or for ill."

"But he didn't tell me anything really."

The logbook snapped shut so hard that the boy jumped back. "Do not lie to me on *my* ship. Understood?"

"Yes, sir."

"Explain to me then why you almost threw your life away in such a foolish manner."

"I've got to get down to Washington, sir."

"Why?"

"I . . . I can't tell you. I'm sorry."

The captain stared at him. "Does it have anything to do with the missing brother Mr. Gooden told me about?"

"No!" He glanced at the floor. "Yes."

The captain studied Caleb closely. "You want to look for him, is that it?"

Caleb nodded.

The captain's fingers drummed on the desk. "It is a bad habit aboard ship to answer a question in anything but words. At sea, one can't always look about and see the answer."

"Yes, sir, that's the reason."

"Ah. It's what the bosun thought. But then, let me ask you this: What makes you think you can . . . ?"

Caleb's face suddenly darkened at the thought of having to mention that lie about his brother!

A gleam of light flickered in the captain's eyes. "What makes you think," he began again, "that you can . . . walk about my ship barefoot?"

Caleb shot him a look of gratitude and looked down at his feet. "Sorry."

"I hope you don't mind wearing the socks and shoes of a dead man. After we buried him at sea, he had no one ashore to claim his belongings. We were going to donate them to the old sailors home in Boston, but to shorten this voyage, I decided to make fewer stops."

"Uh . . . how did he die?"

The captain cracked a thin smile. "Nothing you can catch, young man." He studied Caleb a while longer. "There are no idle hands aboard this vessel. Do you feel fit enough to help out the cook in the galley?"

"Aye, sir. But I've been on boats all my life. You can send me up in the rigging or put me to anything!"

"That right? Very tempting. We don't get too many able and willing lads on merchant ships these days. Not since President Lincoln's call for over three hundred thousand army volunteers. Each town's been told how many men it's expected to send. They're all outdoing each other with bigger gifts of cash to anyone who'll claim he's from their town and sign up there.''

"My brother didn't take any gifts to go and fight!" Caleb said heatedly.

"I believe you. No offense intended. But don't use that tone with me. And as for taking you on as a regular seaman, the problem is you're underage. I can't do it without your father's say-so, especially now with raiders on the loose and the navy doing so little to stop them.''

"I ain't afraid of any rebels, pirates or not!" declared the boy.

The captain frowned so deeply that his brow almost came down to his mustaches. "But a grown man would be,'' he said quietly, then fell silent. "Well, when we reach New York, I can decide whether to telegraph your father for permission or just put you ashore there with the price of a train ride. You'll earn that in the galley.''

"But, Captain!" Caleb knew already what answer his father would telegraph back.

There was a flash of annoyance. "You say you've been on boats all your life, yet you argue with the skipper? By the way, I can't have you tying up sick bay anymore. You'll sleep up forward with the men until we make port in a couple of days.''

Standing quickly, the captain went to a door that opened onto the higher of two decks. In the middle of it stood a seaman at the helm. A much taller man was leaning over the poop-deck rail, giving orders to a line of men on the lower deck to hoist one of the sails.

The captain called to him. "Mr. Davis! I need you.''

As the tall man turned around, the captain said, "Take this lad to the forecastle. Get him settled in a bunk and into the sea clothes of that man we lost last voyage. He's to assist the cook until I decide what to do with him.''

"Come along, boy," said Davis, already starting down the short ladder to the deck from which the ship's three masts rose like towers to sway against the sky.

"In case you don't know why the captain calls me Mister," he said while waiting for Caleb to follow him down, "I'm the first mate. But to you I am like God. Which means that I don't care what your age is, it's me you'll get the whipping of your life from if you cause any trouble. Always mind you don't trip over anything on the deck. Stay below if the sea acts up. And watch your step with the men, 'cause there's always a wrong one in every bunch. If someone who's too big for you to lick hits you, fight him back anyway. Fight or take without a blubber what he dishes out until he stops. You don't want to give these bozos any reason to not take you seriously. I'm telling you right, boy. All this from my own experience.''

None of this advice was news to Caleb, who had learned from Grandpa years ago what to expect aboard a seagoing vessel. They had stepped past the mizzenmast in the rear and were coming up to the main, in the center. Here, men were forming a line at a long rope and starting to pull the topgallant royal into place. There were sails over sails on every mast, and now the highest and farthest seen of them all would be catching the wind to add on speed. When the men who were hauling struck up a song he knew, Caleb's own hands began to twitch and his lips to silently repeat the words:

"Old Loocy was the King of France
Before the Revolution
Way! Haul away! We'll haul away Joe.

But then he got his head cut off
Which spoiled his constitution
Way! Haul away! We'll haul away Joe
Oh way, haul away in fair and stormy weather . . ."

The hard-faced Davis almost smiled. "Itching to join them, are you?"

"Yes, sir."

"O-ho! So you fancy yourself one of us already, then?"

Caleb didn't answer, but the first mate laid a hand on his shoulder that was as big and powerful as a grizzly bear's and guided him on to a low-lying cabin just forward of the next mast ahead.

There were two entrances to it, although one was little more than an upright hatch. Right behind this hatch, a ladder went steeply down to the bunks. Davis called from the top, "Men, you'll make room for this lad. He gets the stuff of that fellow we sent to the bottom. And I mean his seaboots, Sou'wester, oilskin coat, socks—all of it. Don't let me catch any of you holding out on him or trying to make him pay for anything." He left the boy there to go down the ladder alone.

There had been some talking below, but all of that stopped the moment Caleb's feet touched the floor of the damp and crowded cabin. Except for the rolling waves outside, the only sound he heard was the creak of a swaying oil lamp. Turning from the ladder, he saw rows of double bunks and men sitting on them sideways, their feet dangling. Some of them were holding mugs in one hand and biscuits called hardtack in the other. They had been dunking the biscuits in their soup, but now they weren't moving. There were so many eyes on him at the

38

same time that Caleb took only one step into the narrow space between the bunks, then stopped.

Standing between the kettle of steaming soup and the open chest of biscuits, he tried to avoid the faces of the men as he looked for an empty berth. But they were making him very uneasy. What was going on here?

Beneath the hanging lamp was a wooden table where a man sat playing cards by himself. He put down the cards and said in a very suspicious voice, "Where do youse come from, boy? We all know youse got on in Maine, but don't hand us no garbage that you're a down-easter. I never once shipped with a Maine man who knew how to swim. They always tell ya seawater is only for lobsters. So as young and innocent like as youse look, what I think is you're a rebel spy." He slapped down his cards. "Now what do youse say to *that?*"

Without waiting for an answer, the fellow got to his feet and closed in. He was very small for a grown man, and not much heavier than Caleb. But he looked as hard as rock, and his jaw stuck out like a challenge. His eyes had the look of someone who was never satisfied unless he could find some reason to be angry. And from beneath the left eye a nasty scar slanted down across his cheek until it lost itself in the braided hair behind his neck.

A stab of fear plunged so deeply into the boy's gut that it took most of his breath away. He had to stand up to this man. But what if he couldn't get the words out? He forced them. "I say that you don't know what you're talking about!"

Several of the men had been chuckling. So far they hadn't been taking the ribbing of this boy seriously. But now they sensed that this wasn't a game any longer.

"What's that? What's that?" snapped the man wildly.

"Youse must be lookin' to have your head broken off, right there!" Balling a fist, he raised it to the boy's face.

Caleb knew this wouldn't be like any fight he'd ever had with another schoolboy. But his arms felt so heavy. And yet if he didn't act *fast* . . .

From an upper of a bunk came a sleepy voice. "You had your little fun, Shiprat. Back into your hole now."

"Who called me that?" screeched the man. His head swiveled around, his hair braid flew. "Who called me Shiprat?"

"Somebody who knows one when he meets one. Joshua Gooden."

"Oh youse," the little man spat out. "Well, I don't see that what I do or don't do is any business of yours now that youse ain't our bosun no more. You're just pulling the same wages as the rest of us, feller."

"That's no skin off your nose, bub. This boy's folks opened their home to the crew of my last ship after she went down. Fed us good and got their whole town to pitch in. That's something I won't ever forget."

A murmur of approval went through the forecastle. It left the bully cut off from any backing.

"Well . . . well why didn't youse tell us all that in the first place then?" he grunted, backing off.

"Maybe it's 'cause I was sleeping till you woke me. Or maybe I was just waiting to see which are the fools I'm shipping out with this run and who are the real men. This here is Caleb Peasley, of a seagoing family, boys. And I mean to see him treated fair. You all right, Caleb?"

"Yes, I'm fine, Joshua. Thank you."

Now one of the other men spoke up softly. "Hey, I seen you was stepping kind of funny down the ladder. Frostbite on your feet?"

40

Caleb answered with a shrug, though it was beginning to worry him. "Maybe some."

"Be they numb or tingling?"

"Tingling."

"Oh, well, that's a good sign. Shows they're getting better. But a thing like that keeps coming back when you get enough chill. Watch out for it."

"That's a good one, that is!" snorted another man. "How does anybody watch out when the wind's out of the north and the sea is up?"

"I'll be all right," said Caleb.

"All that milk o'human kindness, but I don't hear any offers," said Joshua Gooden, leaning over the side of his top bunk. "How's about someone down there switching to an upper so he don't have to climb for a bit?

A sailor who had been laying back reading a book swung up from his lower bunk. "Take this one."

Caleb stared at him. He'd never seen a black man before.

The man stared back. "Or perhaps you don't want my bed?"

"Oh, I'll take it! Thanks."

"Hey, Fish," called the shiprat, who was still smarting. "Let's see how well you fill a dead man's boots."

The boots came flying at Caleb. He caught one, but the other bounced off a post.

"You dumb fool!" somebody cried, and jumped down from his bunk ready to throw himself upon the man. "That could have gone into the soup."

"Well, I'd try anything to improve the taste!" the black man said quickly before a fight could start. Laughter exploded everywhere, and it ended the quarrel.

*   *   *

Caleb was still pretty weak, and when he sank into his bunk, he quickly fell asleep again. He was awakened by someone shaking him. "This is my bunk now, brother," said a man coming off his deck watch.

The boy sat up, rubbing his eyes, and realized he had yet to report for duty at the galley. Back up the ladder and out the hatch he went, then walked around the very same low-lying cabin to the kitchen's step-down entrance on the opposite. As he did so, he had to walk past excitable chickens who flung themselves at him but couldn't get past the wire fence that cooped them up against a wall.

The cook was standing in front of his door, wringing the neck of a bird. "Wo Fong most happy to see you," he said, pushing the wildly flapping fowl into the boy's hands. "Finish. Pluck feathers. Make clean. Do one bird more."

He hated—absolutely hated—this task. Hauling in a big salmon or chasing a flopping fish across the *Indian Maiden*'s deck never felt like killing in the same way that this did. Plucking the chicken afterward, although some boys he knew thought of this as "women's work," didn't bother him. It reminded him of a time when his grandmother was alive and geese were kept outside the house. He'd help her pluck the feathers before a goose was roasted. Then he'd sit down at the table and pull out the stems. What was left went into new pillows and quilts, and Caleb always had the feeling he'd been a part of the process of making them.

The birds were for the officers' table. Caleb did other chores while they were being cooked. Afterward, Wo Fong had him clean himself up, then serve the meal to the captain and the ship's two mates at a table in the skipper's chart room up on the bridge deck. Everything

42

went smoothly as he set out the food, waited quietly out of sight while everyone ate, then picked up the empty dishes to bring them back to the galley. After he put them down in the sink, Wo Fong sent him out with a steaming pot of coffee. This was a bit tricky because the sea had been growing rough. He was carefully carrying it across a rolling deck when a sailor standing nearby suddenly shouted at him, *"Heads up!"*

Caleb just had time to see the falling mallet come straight at him and to spring to the side. The heavy metal tool hit the deck with a force that could have cracked his skull. He was too shaken for the moment to feel the scalding pain of coffee running down the leg of his trousers.

"Oh, sorry!" piped a voice from somewhere above that was half a happy cackle.

Joshua Gooden came away from his work to stare up at the rigging. "Shiprat, I saw you do that on purpose!"

"That ain't my name," screamed the man, leaning down from a wooden crosspiece on the topsail of the center mast. "And youse didn't see nothing but a mistake. That's all youse saw!"

The cook had apparently seen it, too. When Caleb came back for more coffee, Wo Fong made him take his pants off and handed him a clean cloth with greasy ointment on it that the boy had never seen before. While the boy spread the soothing cream over his blistering skin, Wo Fong cleaned the pant leg with a wet rag. Then, warning him in his terribly broken English to be more careful, he handed him a refilled pot of coffee and sent the boy off.

"You seem to be limping," the captain said as he went back into the dining room. "Did you hurt yourself?

"No, I'm fine, sir. It isn't anything."

The captain went back to his conversation with the

ship's officers. "I've been thinking," said the second mate, toying with his cup, "that the navy's given us those two cannons, but nobody's practiced using them yet."

"I wouldn't take a chance on it," explained the captain, leaning back to light his cigar. "That's like sending out an announcement of our position. No, our best ally is the silence."

"And our speed as well," said the first mate. "With this following wind, we're doing better than twelve knots. Be hard for anybody to match it."

"Sure, but we won't be making that once we have a heavy cargo in our holds. And considering what we'll be carrying, you'd think the government would send a frigate to guard us the rest of the way."

"What? To watch over just one ship?" said the captain, leaning back to light his cigar. "The navy's much too spread out blockading the southern coast all the way from Virginia to Mexico."

"Well, they could bunch up a few cargo ships to go down at the same time and send a frigate to guard *that*."

"Pipe dream, I'm afraid," said the captain. "Some of us have been suggesting the same thing for over a year and getting nowhere."

The second mate's spoon rattled against the table. "But hang it all, Captain. If they ever set fire to the number one hold, why this ship wouldn't last two minutes!"

"I ask you to mind yourself!" said the captain sternly. "There are a very lively pair of ears besides our own in this cabin."

"That's all right, sir," Caleb said quickly. "I'm not afraid of anything."

The captain gazed at him thoughtfully. "No grown man would say that. Certainly not think it."

Caleb realized it had been a mistake to speak up. He felt the captain's eyes upon him as he finished going round the table, refilling the cups. He sensed what was coming before the words were even spoken.

"Son, I've given this some thought, and I've come to a decision. Whether your father would give his consent or not, I'm leaving you ashore in New York. Too young."

With Caleb's heart already sinking, he gave it one last try. "But I've heard there are drummer boys in the army who aren't much older than I am."

"Is that what you mean to do when you get there? Join up so you can look for your brother?"

"Well . . . I . . . I was thinking about it."

"Then that's another reason why I can't take you. No, I won't have any part in your taking such risks. This is settled."

Caleb trudged back to the galley with his head drooping. He was just about to enter it when the door cracked open just wide enough for him to hear voices.

"Well, of course I would like to have you read these poems," Wo Fong was saying. "But it would be more useful to hear your opinion after I finish polishing my translation."

"Yes, I'm looking forward to that, my friend. But this question has been on my mind, and I really have to ask you straight out. Why do you hide your education like this from everyone but me? Why talk in broken English?"

"I am very surprised you haven't guessed yet, Steven, knowing how your own race is treated."

"Well, I have in a way, but . . ."

"It's very simple. When I use my pidgin English, they only make fun of me. Then I am just a silly Chinaman, and as long as they are laughing at me, they don't resent me enough to harm me. Yet you, Steven Duval, a black man, you're in a more dangerous situation than I. There are some aboard this ship who hate *your* people even more than mine because a war is now being fought over them. The first thing that goes wrong on this voyage and they will take it out on you.''

"I understand what you say, Wo Fong. But I didn't escape from my master ten years ago in order to shuffle about as if I was still a slave.''

Caleb heard Wo Fong sigh, then say, ''Well, I see there's no warning you.''

"But you tried, my friend. And I appreciate it.''

The door now swung wide open. And the black sailor, coming out, found himself face to face with the open-mouthed boy. He gave Caleb a searching look, then merely nodded and moved on.

But the cook had seen Caleb, too. His eyes popped, and he began to fume. ''Boy, why you sneak around? No wait dinner finish, bring back plates, chop, chop?'' Before Caleb could reply, the cook had worked himself up even more. ''No more Wo Fong need you here. You no good! Go other place plenty fast!''

"But . . .''

"No tell Wo Fong some 'but'.'' Snatching up a bread knife, he rushed the door, waving the knife over his head.

Caleb fell back and took a few moments to collect himself after the cook retreated into his galley. Then more depressed than ever, he headed toward the men's quarters. But just beyond it, he saw Steven Duval standing by the port rail near the bow, gazing into the night. Caleb hesitated a few moments, then went over.

"Mr. Duval?''

"So you know my name. You did hear us talking.''

"But I couldn't help it. Can you tell me please what I did wrong?"

"Nothing. Well, that depends on what you heard."

"Wo Fong warning you. And how he really speaks. And his saying why he talks the other way. But that sounds crazy."

"Maybe not so crazy." Duval interrupted himself to point. "Look how lovely that is."

A gull with its wings spread wide was soaring across the face of the moon. Caleb waited until Duval began again. "Wo Fong has a large family to feed back in San Francisco, and they are having very bad times. Once he was wealthy, but all the gold he dug out of the mountains was taken from him by a gang of white vigilantes who beat him and left him for dead. He would lose his job if one or two ignorant sailors started any trouble."

"Why wouldn't the captain just get rid of the men who bothered him?"

"Because, except for me, the rest of the crew would walk off the ship. Either that or blame Wo Fong for causing trouble. And on a night just a little darker than this, he'd fall overboard."

Caleb looked at the book of Shakespeare's plays in the sailor's hand. "So was Wo Fong right when he said what people might do to you?"

The sailor shrugged and fell silent again. Caleb reached for his pocket watch, then recalled how salt water had ruined it. He glanced up to read the position of the Big Dipper. Give or take a few minutes, it was close to eight o'clock.

At last he said, without looking at the man, "If anyone tried something like that, I'd help you."

"Would you, now?"

47

"Yes, I would."

Then he smiled. "And why would you do a thing like that?"

Caleb shrugged. He had never felt good about answering a lot of questions. But finally he said, "Because, fair's fair."

"Well, I guess it is."

There was another silence. "My grandfather freed all the people in a slave ship. Over a hundred of them."

The sailor swung halfway around to look at him. "You don't tell me?"

"Yes, I do," the boy declared with a touch of pride.

"I've read of a slave who did the same thing, and forced the ship's pilot to take them all back to Africa."

That was one better than his grandfather had done. "Gramps had to set them down on an island," Caleb said heavily. Then he brightened. "But it had plenty of food and water!"

"Good for him. And it's a wonderful story."

"It's true!"

"I certainly hope so. Well, so the captain made you a cabin boy?"

"Wo Fong fired me."

"He'll change his mind."

"Doesn't matter," the boy replied unhappily. "Captain says I have to get off in New York. I'm not old enough."

Caleb stopped feeling like talking at all. But neither did he feel like going down to his bunk. His companion had no desire to go anywhere, either. Little by little they started telling about their lives. Somewhere southeast of Boston, Caleb told Steven Duval of the lie about his brother.

And very late that night, somewhere close to Long Island Sound, a plan was formed.

48

4

It was a rainy morning when the *Dolphin* rounded Coney Island to turn into New York's harbor. The huge bay was filled with vessels going in and out—most of them without sails and belching smoke from their stacks. The ship ran down its sails as it drew near to the city. Then, with the help of a tug, it docked at a wharf in front of a great military warehouse inside the navy yard.

When the gangplank was lowered, the captain came down from the bridge to leave the ship. First though, he slipped a few dollars into Caleb's pocket, saying, "Best of luck to you." But the boy felt so badly about having to trick the man that he barely pressed back when they shook hands.

He lingered on board, then left the ship when nobody was particularly watching. Now he walked slowly toward the big fence at the far end of the yard. It was very important, Steven had told him, not to go through it, past the guard post. "You'd never get back, at least not without being shot."

Along the way there was a broken-down shed to look out for. Steven, who had worked in this place, remembered that empty metal drums and rusting bits of ships' tackle had been stored there. Caleb spotted it off to his left, behind the yard's commissary. Drifting that way with others who were going to buy something to eat or wear, he slipped around the building, ducked low, and made a dash for the shed.

He'd known ahead of time that there'd be a long wait before his friend could come for him. But after hours of crouching there, he realized what a mistake it had been to bring nothing to eat but hardtack. They were very dry to start with, and when the gray rats came out to sniff at him, his mouth became too dry to swallow. He didn't dare make a racket to chase them away—and even if he had tried, they might not have gone. They were big as cats, they watched with shining eyes, and their mouths quivered each time he tried to chew. Caleb had long ago learned that rats were smart. The only way to get rid of them was turn his pockets inside out and throw all the biscuits out of the shed, hoping no one would see him do it. Nobody did.

The day passed; evening came. Sounds of carts and of hoists and of grunting men loading ships died away. More hours passed while the sky, visible through the holes in the roof, thickened into night. Then Duval came silently in the blackness, with an empty seabag. Caleb stepped into it and squatted while the bag closed over him. He felt himself being lifted—heard a surprised gasp of pain—and was dropped. There was heavy breathing, then he was lifted again. Lying across Duval's back, he could hear the heavy scrape of shoes as the man staggered away.

"Listen, put me down. Forget about it."

"Keep quiet," Duval whispered back furiously. "It's

been a long time since I've carried loads like this. But I have the feel of it now. We'll make it.''

They went on until Caleb heard the boards of the *Dolphin*'s gangplank, and they started to go up its slope. He heard a deep breath and felt his friend straighten up as if to make the seabag look too light to take notice of.

Yet a voice on deck—it belonged to the first mate— asked, ''What have you got in there, Duval? I thought your gear was already aboard.''

''Oh, it is,'' the sailor replied easily. ''These are some things I bought at the commissary to take to my aunt's family in D.C. Everything is very scarce down there. And even when you can find what you need in the stores, why the prices are too high for any person who cleans other people's houses to pay. Do you want to look inside?''

''No. None of my business as long as you can find a place to stow what you've got out of the way. Best be careful, though, lest someone wants to take it from you.''

''I'll be all right,'' said Duval, moving on. ''Thanks.''

''All the same, I'd watch out for the shiprat. Mean and sneaky ones like him have always got a knife out for the colored folk.''

Crossing the deck, Duval carried him into the galley and set him down. The cook, watching Caleb rise out of the bag, waved a skillet and went into his usual act. ''I no want. Him trouble. Why you bring boy here?''

''He already knows how well you speak, Wo Fong.''

''How wonderful that you've brought me a stowaway!'' said the cook gloomily. ''What if they discover him?''

''I won't tell anybody that you hid me.''

''Me? Hide you? But where? That's impossible.''

''No one but you goes into the pantry,'' Duval reminded him.

51

"That is all changed as of today. The captain took on a steward. He'll have his own key, so that if any of the officers get hungry during the night . . ."

Duval scratched his head. "The trouble with putting him under the canvas of one of the longboats is that if the mate holds inspection . . ."

Wo Fong perked up. "But that man never climbs up to the one on my roof. He was raised on an egg farm, and now he hates the smell of chicken coops."

Caleb remained in the galley, hidden in a cabinet while the ship got underway. All hands were on deck to run up its sails. And like a ghost in the night, it slid out of the harbor without any running lights. At last the decks were clear of everyone but the man at the helm and the second mate, who was walking up and down on the bridge.

Duval went up to the ship's officer with a question that turned his gaze away from the direction of the galley. Now there was only the helmsman for Caleb to worry about when he darted out the door and began to climb to the roof. But the gaze of the man guiding the ship was fixed on the darkness ahead, and Caleb ducked to safety under the dory's canvas covering. Sometime later on, Wo Fong pretended to busy himself repairing the wire and the top of a coop. As he raised himself up on a stool, he handed the boy a jar of water, a little package of food, and a bucket, which he said was for "doing your business."

All this kindness and help gave Caleb a warm feeling that not even the chill of night could chase away. He sat on the floor of the boat thinking that he had good friends. That he was on his way. And even though he was doing this for his brother, it was an adventure, too!

5

The boredom got to him. There were days of doing nothing in his hiding place under the canvas tarp but shifting from sitting to lying and back again among the ribs of the small boat. He invented stretches to keep from cramping up and exercises to work off energy. But it was easier to deal with his body than with certain thoughts that ran through his brain. The hardest of these concerned his folks and what his running away must have done to them. He could picture his mother worrying about having two sons now to lose in the war and see the deeper tremble in the corners of her mouth.

But then, what else could he have done but to go and try to find Jonathan? They would have stopped him if they could, that's true. And yet, wasn't this just the sort of thing his grandfather would have done himself if he'd been young? Why, it was as natural as blueberries that Gramps would!

So the only real thing to think about now, he told himself, was "*Where is my brother?* Maybe he's wandering around somewhere with his memory gone, like that man Gramps told about once, the captain of a whaler. A harpooner's hook had gone into his skull, and right off he forgot who his family was and where he lived. He even had to be taught again like a child how to speak English!''

Yes, but what about the terrible thing those returning soldiers had said about Jonathan? How had that lie started? It was a question that had no answer. Whenever he slept, it nagged at the edges of his dreams; and finally it brought him a nightmare.

His brother was lying on his face on that dark hillside in Fredericksburg. Sounds of laughter came from the rebel lines above. If those men were so free and easy, Jonathan told himself, it was because they felt safe. And why shouldn't they when there were so many thousands of them up there. But here there was only his regiment— and all these Union corpses! Suddenly, before he even knew what he was doing, Jonathan was on his feet screaming, "For God's sake, Colonel, get ourselves out of here! Our whole army is back across the river!''

The sweating dreamer knew beforehand what the colonel was going to call his brother! He dreaded to hear that word. He didn't want to hear that terrible word!

He was rescued from the dream by the ship's first mate shouting an order. He awakened to the sounds of a rising wind and of men racing to the ropes that worked the sails. The *Dolphin* had begun to pitch heavily, and sailors of the watch that had been off duty stomped out of the forecastle, still pulling on their seaboots. Caleb heard shouts only a few feet below where he hid. "Looks like the captain wants our backs to the blow.''

"Aye, but that gets us farther away from land. And the rebs are thick out here.''

"It's giving us speed, matey.''

"Not if the main mast goes down," warned a third voice that Caleb recognized. "Look how she's swaying. Something's wrong with one of the stays. And if it snaps, other ropes will, too."

"I wouldn't worry about it, Gooden. She's held in worse blows that this."

"Ah, ye think so, do ye? This here particular blow is going to go round us like a clock to box the compass. Look there at the sky, how it's getting lighter. Wind's going to fall off soon enough from that quarter. Then it'll come at us with the shock of death from the other direction."

"If you know all this, man, why don't you tell the mate on your watch?"

"He wouldn't want to hear it from an ordinary seaman is why."

The ship's bells began to ring out. From the poop deck came a new command "All hands to the ropes!" And conversation ended.

Knowing what was coming, Caleb searched for the best way to protect himself from being dangerously tossed about inside the dory. The best he could manage was to tie his arms around a seat and brace his feet against another. The seas, meanwhile, quickly rose. The *Dolphin* pitched, tossed, reared up on its stern like a bucking horse, and crashed bow first into a deep emptiness between towering waves. Through all of this he held on—and was still holding when the gale suddenly stopped. Caleb caught his breath. The stillness was eerie.

And then it came. Gooden had been right about the change of direction—and even more right about the shock. The wind hit with a power that made thick timbers shudder. Its sound was like sea-witches shrieking as it whistled through the masts and tore at the sails. And this time, the waves came on like foaming mountains. They broke high over the deck with enough fury to carry any man clear across it and over the far side. But the sailors clung to the rails, the lifelines, whatever they could get hold off. And Caleb, as drenched as any of them on the deck below, held on, too.

Pffft! Something had snapped and went whipping off into the wind. There was another snapping sound and another, followed by a dreadful straining creak and a sudden dreadful crack, like a great tree breaking in half.

''The mast! The mast!'' men howled.

Caleb yanked free of the tarp, saw the mast coming down at him, and . . . *nothing.* Missing the dory entirely, the falling mass of wood and sail crashed nearby, taking part of the port rail with it. It hung out over the sea, dangerously tipping the ship and making her impossible to steer. Wave after wave broke over the deck in great waterfalls. Yet the men worked frantically to free the broken mast from its tangle of ropes, sails, and tackle and haul it back in.

Caleb, sloshing around in the water that had gotten into his lifeboat, longed to join them. Doing nothing to help was the worst prison sentence he could imagine. His impatience wore him out so badly that as the storm came to an end at last, he fell into a dizzying sleep. It was then, for a second time, that he dreamed of the battle of Fredericksburg.

Once again an officer jumped up to scream in panic about getting out of there. Once again the colonel called out to arrest the ''traitor.'' But this time the soldier wasn't Jonathan Peasley. It was Caleb. ''You're wrong!

I can't be!" he screamed back at them. "I am not a traitor!"

And yet . . . and yet . . . he had started to run away. He didn't want to run away! He told himself to stop, but he couldn't stop! His feet were disobeying him! He roared orders at his feet. "Turn, turn the other way! Turn—"

Someone grabbed him by the shoulder, shook him, and harshly whispered, "Wake up and be silent!"

His eyes flew open. He was in the dory. He saw an arm draw away and the worried, disappearing face of Wo Fong.

Had anybody else heard him cry out in his sleep? He lay there breathlessly, but all seemed well. He was just starting to breathe normally again, when a great blast brought sleeping men pouring out of the forecastle.

He heard Shiprat croak, "What's up? What's going on?"

"We've just had one across the bow."

"One of what?"

"A cannonball, matey. Are you deaf?"

"No, I ain't deaf. In this dark, I don't see nothing. Where's it comin' from?"

"Look into the wind. You'll see it plain enough when the next one flashes."

"But how do they see us, is what I'm askin'!" piped the little man. "There's only one way. And that's 'cause there's a spy aboard of this ship. Somebody what's got hold of a piece of glass daytimes and a lantern at night. Somebody what flashes our position. And now that we're movin' so slow on account of the mast . . ."

"You got spies on the brain," grunted the first man.

57

"Think it over. He'd be in the same bowl of soup as the rest of us if the ship blows up."

"My God! My God!" screamed Shiprat. "If one of them balls hits us midship, we're done for!"

"Rockets!" someone shouted. "She's showing herself!"

Lifting an end of the canvas, Caleb saw the sky flame into light above the sails of a three-mast schooner, slender as a new-fangled cigarette and built for speed. At the same time, another cannon boomed. The shot went overhead and sent water spouting over the *Dolphin*'s far side.

Now a signal light began to flash at them.

"Can anybody read that?"

"Don't have to," said Joshua Gooden grimly. " 'Tis a signal I've seen once before. They're ordering us to surrender or go down."

A sharp whistle drew everyone's attention to the bridge deck. It was the captain himself calling orders. "Men, we're bringing out muskets with fixed bayonets, and enough cartridges to put up a good fight. The mates will work the cannon. We'll wait until they draw near to board us—and give better than we get. Remember this is for our country!"

Standing just below the dory, Shiprat began wildly laughing. "What?" he jeered. "We're gonna pretend to fight a ship o'war, are we? And us with a cargo that'll blow us to kingdom come! Are we crazy? Shipmates, we don't stand a chance here! Let the captain play at being a hero! Me for the lifeboats! Who'll help me get this dory into the water?"

"Stow that talk!" roared Joshua Gooden, limping along the deck. "Nobody's abandoning ship—not even the rats."

"Youse ain't no bosun. Shut your face, or I'll give youse a taste of this!"

"Put the knife away," Gooden growled darkly.

"Sure, I'll put it in you . . . right up to the hilt."

Caleb heard Steven Duval speak up in his calming voice. "If we fight among ourselves, shipmates, we're lost at the start."

"Don't youse call me your shipmate!" the little man hissed. "If it wasn't for all youse blacks, there wouldn't be no war and this wouldn't be happenin' to us!"

Caleb heard scuffling, then a groan. He tore at the canvas, saw Duval stagger, holding his side. Caleb grabbed the side of the long boat just as Shiprat closed in again on his falling victim. The boy leaped—and Shiprat went down to his knees under him. But there was enough power in the little man's coiled body to fling Caleb off, then whirl round to face him, his zigzagging knife slicing air. Caleb sprang back, but the galley wall blocked him. There was no escape from that long and weaving blade, already dripping blood.

No one was ready to take on the knife-wielding man, but there were murmurs of "Let him be."

"Sure I will!" snorted Shiprat. "I'll save him so them rebs can give him a medal! All o'youse thought we'd got rid of him, but all o'youse was wrong. He had to come sneakin' back aboard of this ship to signal the enemy. He was hidin' up there where the Chinaman could stand watch while he did it!"

"You ain't thinking straight, matey. Why would Cookie do a thing like that?"

"Why? Youse ask me why? Them Chinamen, they hate all of us whites, and they wants us to kill each other off. What did I tell youse the first day about this here kid! I knew it from the start that he was a spy. He doomed this ship, and I'm gonna finish him forever.''

The knife jabs came closer now—and still no one was moving to save Caleb. He went weak in the legs. He sagged. His ears rang. His eyes swam till even that knife became a blur. *Face dying!* he screamed at himself. *Face it or be a coward!*

There was a loud crack, and Shiprat's arms suddenly flew out at his sides. The gunshot from the bridge caught the man between the shoulder blades—and sent him spinning into an iron post.

Caleb's eyes were still blinking when two sailors scooped Shiprat from the post and brought him to the side where the rail was gone. ''Say hello to the sharks, matey,'' one of them grunted, and they heaved him overboard.

''Get that wounded man to sick bay,'' barked the second mate, lowering his smoking musket.

Duval was on the deck, unconscious and bleeding badly from the left side. Caleb lifted the man's right arm over his shoulder and got him halfway to his feet. Gooden took the other arm, while a big man lifted the feet. Carrying Duval up to the poop deck, they went through the chart house and set him down on top of the sick-bay bed.

The captain left his first and second mates handing out guns. He gave the boy a sweeping look as he hurried inside but said nothing until he undid Duval's shirt. ''My God, look at all the blood! This is wide and looks deep. But I can't stop now to sew it up, even if that could save him.''

He turned to the boy. ''Use the bedsheet if you need to, to hold back the bleeding. But I don't think it will help.'' He hurried to a cabinet. ''Here's a bottle of whis-

key to make his dying easier, if he wakens. I'm sorry."
As he turned to go, Wo Fong entered, holding a tray.
"Captain—" the cook began.

But the captain bellowed in his face, "What kind of
a fool are you? We're about to be boarded and have
our throats slit, and you think this is the time to serve
me breakfast!"

"No, sir, I do not," Wo Fong replied quietly. "Nor
am I well versed in surgery, but I do have some skills
in preventing infection that are not commonly known.
May I show you these ointments and how to apply
them?"

The skipper's mouth dropped open. "Well, I'll be
hornswoggled!"

"Captain!" Vezzings, the second mate rushed in, a
spyglass in his hand. "Something's wrong with the
enemy ship! She's listing."

"Wo Fong, I leave this man to you!" The captain
rushed away.

"The rest of you go, too," said Wo Fong. "Boy, bring
me boiling water. Hurry!"

As Caleb raced through the chart room and across the
poop deck to the ladder he heard the mate say, "My
guess is that ship's been patched together too many times
to take the kind of weather we just had. Split a seam
wide open probably, and taking on more water than her
pumps can push out again. She'll go under in an hour
or two."

"Then that's how long her captain has to capture us
and transfer his crew."

"Aye, but if the man's turned pirate and wants to save
a bit of money, we won't even be treated as prisoners of

war. He'll think why feed any of us when we can all be made to disappear without a trace?''

''In that case, we've got nothing to lose if we make a run for it, even with one of our masts broken,'' said the captain thoughtfully.

''Yes, but then the enemy's got nothing to lose either by blowing us out of the water before she sinks. And at this range they can do it.''

Caleb had lost enough seconds listening at the foot of the ladder when his friend could be dying! Racing to the galley, he grabbed a pot of steaming water and rushed back to the poop-deck ladder.

Meanwhile, the captain had come to a decision. ''Signal them, Mr. Davis. Tell their captain that I won't surrender. Nor will I give him any chance to have us boarded. But if he wants to save his crew, he should abandon ship. Let them come over in their lifeboats *unarmed*. They will be treated well.''

Caleb had darted through the chart room just before the first mate entered to get the signal lamp.

''You took too long!'' cried Wo Fong.

Caleb gasped. ''Is he *gone?*''

''No. The bleeding cleaned out some of the gash, but he is very weak. Please, leave me alone now. I must concentrate on what I am doing.''

Caleb was glad to wander out into the chart room. Through the open door to the deck he heard the captain say with relief, ''They are starting to lower boats. Good. We'll keep our men covering them and make them take their clothes off, just to be sure, before coming aboard.''

The first mate was holding the spyglass. Now he pointed. ''I see men diving overboard, Captain.''

"A large crew then, and not enough room. We'll move in a bit closer to pick the swimmers up."

"Skipper, I wouldn't do that!" Davis said anxiously.

"There is no choice. War or no war, we are human beings, after all." The captain called an order to the sailor at the helm. "Hard a-port!"

With his hands on two of its spokes the helmsman swung the big wheel all the way over to the left. "Hard a-port, it is, sir!"

"We're making it easier on the rebs, Captain," the mate warned as the *Dolphin* began to turn its bow towards the men splashing in the icy water. "Look at their ship. It's coming about sideways to give us a full broadside! There's got to be a whole battery of cannons that can fire straight at us now."

"What's wrong with you, mister?" exploded the captain. "Even if they hate us, they can't afford to sink us. We're pulling them out of the sea!"

"Not *all* of them!" cried the mate as six round puffs of fire and smoke appeared at once. Split seconds later came the whine of incoming shells. Two of them burst in the sky. Showers of jagged metal rained down to rip through sails and fall among the men on the main deck. Another shell crashed into the bow and the forecastle without exploding. Panicked men raced up from below. And suddenly the galley's roof burst into fire.

"Man the buckets! Bucket brigade!" roared all three officers at once.

"My God, Captain," yelled the second mate, hurrying to the poop rail. "If that fire reaches the main hold, we'll go up like the Fourth of July!"

"Abandon ship!" some of the sailors were shrieking, but the dory in which Caleb had stowed away was now in flames. That left only one other lifeboat for the entire crew. Pushing, shoving, stumbling men tried to beat each other to it and ended by throwing punches.

Up on the bridge, the captain turned on the officers standing beside him. "Don't just look at those men! Go and make them fight that blaze instead of each other!" The mates hurled themselves down the outside ladder to the main deck. The captain whirled round to shout an order at the helm before hurrying after them. "Bring the ship about, my man! Get us out of the line of fire!"

"Aye, sir," grunted the sailor at the wheel.

But Caleb saw what the captain had not: gushing blood and a jagged slice of metal jutting out from the thick muscles of the helmsman's neck. That brave seaman gave the wheel one hard twist, then he fell over it, slipped sideways, and crashed to the deck.

The boy ran to the spinning helm, caught it by the spokes, and tried to bring it back. But the *Dolphin* was a damaged vessel. He threw all his weight into pulling at that wheel, but it was like trying to lift a boulder; she fought back against moving from one direction to another.

Grandpa Peasley's words flooded back to him. "When you want a ship to really give you what you need, then you've got to talk to her from the heart. No Yankee clipper that's been put together with love was ever just made of wood and canvas. From the moment she's been christened . . . and her keel slips down into the waters for the first time . . . she takes on a soul."

Caleb told the *Dolphin* that he was afraid—afraid for himself and for the others. He said that he was also afraid for *her*. She had been wounded already, but he asked her not to give up. She had a good captain who would do

64

everything he could for her, everything to make her as strong and proud as those wonderful sea creatures she had been named for. What his words did for the ship, he did not know. But they calmed him—and slowly, slowly, he steadied her into the wind.

All this time the cannons had been blasting away at the fleeing ship. Spouts of water rose where shells slammed into the waves on either side. They had been falling close enough, but now one curved down with a whine just behind the stern. When it exploded, the shock wave lifted Caleb like a twig in a hurricane and threw him into the wheel. It was the pit of his stomach that took most of the blow. All the air blew out of him in an instant, and he blacked out.

There was no way of telling whether it was seconds or minutes before his senses returned. Yet one thing was certain, his hands gripped the helm of the *Dolphin*. He was still guiding it to safety.

There was something else that he could be sure of. He was part of the crew now—as important as any of the officers and sailors passing buckets of seawater down the line to be thrown on the fire. Either everyone would live or everyone would die in a single instant. It was all for one and one for all. They were determined to live.

6

It was two days before the *Dolphin* left the ocean behind and headed up the Potomac River to Washington. The vessel was in bad shape. One of her masts was gone, her sails were torn, and her main deck had been scorched by fire. But Old Glory flapped in the breeze as she sailed past Greenleaf's Point to dock at the navy yard.

Within minutes a naval officer came on board to get the skipper's report. When the two men went into the chart room, Caleb, who was sitting with Wo Fong by Duval's bedside next door, could hear their conversation. The captain wasn't interested in talking about his struggle with the Confederate raider. That was over and done with. "What I need to know," he said anxiously, "is how soon will the *Dolphin* go into repair."

"I'm afraid I can't say."

"You *can't* say? You *must* say! I have risked my ship and the lives of my crew keeping my promise to bring the government this cargo. Do you expect me to just sit here for the rest of the war and twiddle my thumbs?"

"The rest of the war could come soon enough," the officer said grimly. "The army's lost another big battle,

I'm afraid, this time at Chancellorsville. And there's fear that Lee will march here now to capture Washington. There are families leaving the city and fleeing north. Some of our best ships' carpenters have gone with them. Now, before I leave, are there any injured men to be taken to a hospital?''

In the sick bay, Duval's lips began to move, but the sounds he made were almost impossible to hear. Both Caleb and Wo Fong bent toward him. ''Don't let me go to a military hospital,'' he pleaded. "If the Confederates take the city, they'll kill any black man who'd fought them.''

Wo Fong, with Caleb behind him, hurried into the chart room, saying, "Captain, I advise against taking Duval off the boat. He's very weak, having lost so much blood. And from what I know of these wartime hospitals, more men get worse in them than better. Cleanliness is unheard of, and the doctors are too tired to see straight!''

"Who is this fellow?'' asked the officer, bewildered.

"My cook.''

"Your . . . your *cook?*''

The captain cracked a much needed smile. Then his gaze came to rest upon Caleb. "But there is something important you can do for me, Commander. You can take that fine young man personally to the War Department and make sure that somebody there takes him seriously. There's been no word of his brother since Fredericksburg, and the lad's come all the way down here to find out.''

"I'll give him a note to show at the desk.''

"A note? Oh, no! From what you've just been telling me, it's likely to be a madhouse over there. Nobody will pay any attention to a boy with a note.''

"All right, then. I'll see what I can do.''

"No," said the captain, striding across the cabin to put a hand on Caleb's shoulder. "I want something better than that. This youngster played a hero's part in saving my ship . . . and the government's cargo."

The officer turned to the boy, got his name, and called out, "Ensign O'Flynn."

"Sir?" A much younger, red-headed officer came in from the poop deck.

"This is Caleb Peasley. The captain tells me he's a hero. I want you to take him directly to the War Department. And no excuses—you are not to leave his side until some officer takes him in hand to help him find his soldier brother. Understood?"

"Aye, sir. I am personally delighted to do anything for a hero." He grinned at Caleb, who winced.

"This will have to satisfy you, Captain," said the commander. "As for me personally, I must see to a hundred other matters before my own ship is finally repaired. Then perhaps I, too, can go back to dealing with the enemy on the high seas. But when that magical day will be, I can't say either."

Caleb had hurried to the door, but the ensign wasn't ready to leave. Instead, he coughed slightly to catch his superior's attention. "I do have a bit of a request, if you don't mind, sir."

"Which is?"

"May I have the use of the commander's horse and buggy, this being such an urgent matter and all? T'would save a good piece of time, what with carriages being so hard to hire down at this part of the city. And a streetcar is hard to come by, sir, as the horses always seem to be pulling away just as a body is running up."

The older officer gave him a long suspicious stare. "Very well," he growled at last. "Off with you."

Caleb waited till they were headed down the gangplank to say, "Look, I'm not the one who said I was any hero."

O'Flynn clapped him on the back. "Ah, in this war everyone's a hero who doesn't run away. Or else plain stupid." His eyes danced merrily. "Did you see the look on the man's poor dumb face when I asked to use his rig?"

"I saw." Caleb returned the grin.

"He loves to prance about in it while pretending he wants to go back to sea. Bought it for a song from some rich widow who was caught spying."

"Was she shot?"

"Oh, no, you don't shoot a lady even after she's cost the lives of thousands of men. You send her down South to be called a hero."

Caleb studied his freckled face. "How old are you?"

The ensign gave him a sly look. "Twenty is a nice fine age, don't you think, for a junior officer?"

"Really?"

"Well, that depends now. If you go by all the things I've seen and done in the world, I'm really quite ancient."

"If I go by that one whisker on your chin, you look seventeen, if that."

They were coming to the horse and buggy. "Goes to show," O'Flynn said as they climbed in, "that you can't tell anything just by the hair on the chinny chin chin. Besides, I had two years fighting Barbary pirates for the British Navy, so the Yanks were glad enough to have me." He shook the reins.

"The Barbary pirates were beaten long ago."

"You don't say? Hmm. It's no wonder then we made such short work of them." He returned a smart salute to the sentry who let them pass onto the streets of Washington. A hard shake of the reins sent the horses into a high-stepping trot.

"Tell me, O'Flynn, do you spend all of your time telling lies?"

"Yes, indeed! I'm practicing up for when it's all over to go into politics. And call me Patrick. Now, I don't know about you, but I am ready for a spot of lunch. There's a lovely meal to be had in Willard's Hotel. And you meet all the best people there at the bar. Somebody who may tell me where to look for your brother."

Caleb shook his head. "You were ordered to take me to the War Department."

"And so I was, but let me ask you two questions. The first is: Can you get a decent meal at the War Department? Or any meal a'tall? Not bloody likely. So the second is: Can you find anybody there who knows what he's doing? Other than, I mean, staying as far away as possible from being shot at? And it's no to that one also. So who is going to help you there? But to Willard's, mind you, comes everyone who can keep a secret and everyone who can't."

They had been flying through the streets when a terrible smell seemed to rise out of the ground. "What's that stink?"

" 'Tis the old canal. You wouldn't want to know what's been fillin' it up. And wouldn't you believe they built all these beautiful white sheds for a wounded man's hospital right beside it? Tell me what you can about your brother. He's not listed as killed, nor captured, nor missing in action?"

When Caleb shook his head, the sadness he felt must have been written on his face. "I think," said the ensign, slowing the horses, "we'll forget about that lunch for a while and pull into here."

As they drove past the sheds it seemed that the patients were being emptied out. They saw legless men being carried to waiting hospital wagons. Others were coming out on their own, using crutches. There were blind men feeling their way along with canes. O'Flynn brought the horses to a stop before a low building with a sign over the door saying ADMINISTRATION.

"Wait here," he told the boy, and went inside, taking a writing pad with him. Twenty minutes later, he came out again, murmuring, "I hate this place!" Jumping into the box quickly, he clamped his large jaw shut and they drove off in silence.

Though anxious to ask questions, Caleb stared at the streets. They were passing through a run-down section of town. He saw blocks that were filled only with black people, many of them in rags, many of them had wary looks on their faces.

"Contrabands," declared O'Flynn moodily.

"What does that mean?"

"It's what they call runaway slaves because they were nothing but property when somebody owned them. Mr. Lincoln only abolished slavery in the states that rebelled. But there's still slavery in some of the states that stayed loyal near here . . . and terrible things are still being done to those people."

They passed other streets with broken fences. Here and there Caleb would see an unshaven white face peering out through the slats, then pulling away quickly.

"Deserters," O'Flynn explained. "They're worried

71

about the army's provost guard arresting them. They beg or steal what they can and live like animals.''

"So what are we going *here* for?'' Caleb snapped at him. "My brother isn't one of *them!*"

O'Flynn sped up the horses. "You don't see me stopping do you?''

"Sorry.'' As they traveled on, Caleb said, "You haven't told me a thing about that hospital.''

"Your brother's battle was in December. All of the men in there now are from fighting that came later. And even those poor devils are being moved out to make room for new ones from this last disaster. I was given the names of about twenty other hospitals though that still have men in them from last year.'' O'Flynn paused, and then he added, "There's just one place that's kept people they can't identify and don't know who they are.''

"Is that where we're going?''

O'Flynn nodded. "It's way on the other side of town.'' He fell silent again.

"What's it called?''

"The Insane Asylum.''

Farther along, Caleb heard the rapid *tap tap tapping* of many hammers coming from behind a high stone wall. "What's going on in there?''

"Coffin-makers. They're building those boxes as fast as they can.'' O'Flynn shook the reins harder. "I'd appreciate it if we didn't talk anymore for a while.''

Caleb nodded. He didn't care to talk, either. The streets were getting a bit nicer now. The houses grew bigger and looked freshly painted. They passed a few stands piled high with fruits. And finally they crossed a wide street where everything seemed to change.

"Pennsylvania Avenue,'' declared O'Flynn. "It leads

72

to the President's house up that way and the Capitol down that way. And right across there, where the brick sidewalk starts, why, that's the hotel I was telling you of."

Caleb looked about. He saw carriages and shops and well-dressed people walking along arm in arm, as if they were out for an Easter stroll. Farther on, a man turned the handle of an organ while a monkey on a string jumped about to the music it played. Two little girls held hands in front of an ice cream cart that stood under the shade of a tree. Other children nearby bounced in impatience while a woman chipped rock candy from a big block.

"Patrick, why are they all so happy and having a good time? I thought we just lost another big battle!"

"Folks get tired of hearing bad news. So do I. You're absolutely sure, now, you don't want me to treat you to the best big breakfast you ever had. We are talking here about baked oysters and steak and onions and some whatnots I'll wager you never heard tell of?"

Caleb shook his head. O'Flynn sighed. They sped on.

The insane asylum was a large wooden building surrounded by high walls. Long ago it had been painted white, but now it was as gray as a sunless day. The boy climbed the front steps slowly, as if he was hanging back out of fear of meeting a ghost. O'Flynn left him sitting on a bench outside the main office, then came back shortly with the assistant director. He was oddly dressed in ruffled clothes out of the time of Benjamin Franklin. He gave Caleb an old-fashioned bow that left the boy wondering if the man himself might be a little mad.

"May I ask you the height and weight of your brother?"

"He's tall."

"How tall, please?"

Caleb lifted a hand about a foot over his own head.

"About six feet then. Yes, and the color of hair?"

"Same as mine."

"Light brown," mumbled the assistant director, leafing through the pages of the folder he carried. When the tracing finger came to a stop midway down one of them, Caleb grew excited. "Jonathan looks a lot like me!"

"Hmm. Yes, now I think about it, there could be some resemblance . . ."

Caleb and O'Flynn exchanged eager glances, but the man rattled on. "Still, one can't be sure. The patients here, I'm afraid, have changed a good deal. Some of them hardly eat and are as thin as rails. Others cram themselves with the food until they become puffy about the face and neck. And with nearly all," he removed his thick glasses, "there is an emptiness about the eyes which is most unfortunate. As a great poet once said, the eyes are the windows of the soul."

"You said there's *somebody* . . ." Caleb reminded him.

"Yes, that is true." When the assistant director paused to close his folder, Caleb almost screamed. "There is one inmate who just *might* fit your brother's description. But you'll need to prepare yourself for a shock."

"Want me to go with you?" O'Flynn asked softly.

"No, but thanks."

Following the assistant director down a long hall, Caleb paused before a large dining room whose doors were wide open. Men in hospital clothes sat on benches at long wooden tables. Some were eating, but very very slowly, as if they weren't aware of what they were doing.

74

Others stared blank-faced at their food, and had to be helped by nuns from the Sisters of Charity.

"He wouldn't be in there," said Caleb's guide leading him away, and the boy breathed a desperate sigh of relief.

Climbing a staircase to the second floor, they went through a pair of swinging doors. The long narrow room had two rows of beds, and all of them were empty. But at the far end was a man in a chair gazing out the window. Unlike the patients downstairs, he seemed unable to sit still. He fidgeted nervously, and his hands trembled. Caleb's heart stopped. He recognized the hair, the shape of the head.

"Jonathan. Jonathan, it's me, Caleb."

At first, the man didn't turn. But his body jolted as if a current of electricity had gone through it.

Caleb felt faint. He reached out to grab the iron railing of a bed. "Jonathan, look at me," he said.

Slowly the head turned. The twitching face came around. A pair of hopeful, wildly searching eyes scanned Caleb's own face, and the man began to stand up.

"Do you know who I am?"

Caleb's voice was so hoarse that he had to repeat himself to be heard. "No," he said breathlessly. "No, I thought you were my— But I was wrong. I'm sorry." The man sank back.

"Well, we tried," sighed O'Flynn minutes later when they were back in the carriage, driving off. "And I do suppose we *could* actually go to the War Department, see what they say. Nothing to lose. What do you think?"

Caleb shook his head. They were coming to the army drill field. He could hear the light rolling of drums.

"So it's back to your shipmates then, is it?"

"Stop here!" said Caleb suddenly.

"What for?"

"You know what for."

The two exchanged glances. "Not on your life!" O'Flynn shook the reins, but before the horses could speed up, Caleb leaped from his seat and tumbled to his knees on the grass.

"Crazy is what you are, boy-o!" O'Flynn reined in the horses. "Come back! You're too young!"

Caleb threw him a grin and started walking backward. "How old I am depends on what I've already seen! Remember?"

As Caleb turned away, O'Flynn tossed the reins aside and jumped down after him. "Forget that blarney and listen to me! You haven't seen anything. One little skirmish at sea is nothing! You don't know war, Caleb! You have no idea!"

The boy whirled round, his eyes brimming with tears. "They called my brother a traitor and a deserter!" Waving his friend back, he broke into a run that didn't stop until he'd crossed the field to a nest of tents.

"Sir!" he cried to a captain coming out of one. "I want to join up!"

The officer peered at him through the smoke of his big cigar. "How old are you, boy?"

Caleb straightened up to give himself more height. "Sixteen."

"Too young, even if you were telling the truth." The captain started to go.

"I want to sign up as a drummer boy."

"Uh-huh. You're not just running away from home to have an adventure?"

"No, sir."

"You're a patriot?"

"Yes, sir."

"You're ready to . . . drum . . . for your country? Bound and determined?"

"Yes, I am, sir."

"Hmm. Your folks will have to give their consent in writing, you know that?"

"I . . . don't have any folks, sir. They're all . . . I'm an orphan."

"That so? Pretty convenient, I should say."

"It's true."

"Who takes care of you?"

"I take care of myself."

"How? How do you make a living?"

"I . . . uh . . . I sell newspapers on the street."

The captain rocked on his heels, then he said, "Go into that tent over there and talk to the sergeant. He does his recruiting at one of the stations in town, but I imagine he'll be delighted to sign you on here. The sergeant won't ask as many questions as I do. There's a promotion in it for him if he can bring in more . . . men."

Caleb found the man sitting in a camp chair in front of a looking glass hanging from a tent pole. The sergeant had but one arm. He was using it at the moment, scissors in hand, to trim a beard that was streaked with gray.

"Welcome, son," he said, giving Caleb a wide smile when he heard why he came. "Do you know how to write?"

"Of course, sir!"

"Good, good. But you don't have to call a sergeant sir. There's the enlistment form on the desk, just under the flap. Pick up that pen and start to write while I finish up here making myself handsome. That's it. Put your name at the top. What is it, by the way?"

"It's . . . William . . . William Strong," said Caleb, writing.

"Strong? Now that's a right smart handle for a brave lad. I see you're having trouble with the next line. You're sure you can read?"

"Yes."

"Then just put down where you're from."

The sergeant took a step closer to lean over his shoulder. "Washington, huh?" He cocked an eye. "Funny. You don't sound to me like you were born in these parts."

"Oh. I didn't say I was born here."

"Right." The sergeant gave him a big wink as Caleb finished the form. Then setting down the scissors, he picked up another question sheet. "Sure wish I could get this over with right quick, but we don't have a doctor here just now to look at you. Oh, well, nobody can read those signatures at the bottom anyways. Why don't you just tell me. How healthy are you?"

"I'm very healthy."

"Stand up right there and let's look at you. Two eyes, two ears, two feet, two hands. Not like me. But I still got my work to do, so I'm not complaining." He slapped down the pad. "Well, Willie, you pass. Congratulations, soldier."

It wasn't until late afternoon that Caleb was actually sworn in. Sent to the quartermaster's big tent, he stuffed his old things in a bag and put on the army uniform a clerk issued him. Nothing felt real to him, though, not even when saw himself in the sergeant's looking glass as he reported back to him.

In some ways this felt much stranger than when he'd run away from home to the seagoing *Dolphin*. Peasleys had been doing just that in one way or another for a couple of hundred years. Also he hadn't really felt he'd left his parents behind, because they'd always be there to come back to. But what about Steven Duval and Wo Fong and Joshua Gooden and the skipper? When would he ever see them again if he didn't do it now?

"Take all the time you want," the sergeant said when asked if he could go off for a few hours before reporting for duty. "But be here at sunup, or I'll shoot you myself."

As Caleb walked back through the city he soon learned why there was no doctor around to examine him. There were horse-drawn ambulances pulling up before large buildings of all kinds that had been turned into hospitals. Some of that traffic had crossed Pennsylvania Avenue going north. But the well-dressed men and women strolling on the brick sidewalk didn't seem to notice. He felt he didn't belong here, and he hurried south toward the river.

The closer to it he drew, the more clogged the road became. This time it was with wounded men who could still walk or stagger along. Their guns and knapsacks were gone. Their faces were caked with mud and dust. Their uniforms were so torn and filthy that Caleb was almost ashamed to be in a clean new one. Many who were limping helped along others who would have fallen. There were those whose heads were covered with bloody rags. These were bitter men, and if they spoke at all, it was in low murmurs.

"Oh dear God in Heaven," exclaimed an old woman standing near Caleb. She grasped his arm. "Look how many of them. Look how many! Is there anyone left who wasn't killed or wounded?"

"Oh, yes, ma'am," a soldier passing by called to her.

"They are still back in Virginia waiting for the next general we get to do the same to them."

When Caleb reached the river, he veered aside and headed for the navy yard. On his way he saw barges coming in, their decks loaded down with the more seriously wounded. The docks were crowded with waiting ambulances, stretcher bearers, doctors, and nurses.

He'd seen enough, and he started to run. He was out of breath when he reached the yard. He walked between huge warehouses to the docks. The *Dolphin* was floating higher in the water now that her cargo was gone. But it hurt him to see that nothing had been done to start repairing that beautiful ship. They owe her that! he told himself, climbing a rope ladder now that the gangplank was gone.

There was no one on deck and no one below it either; the sailors were ashore. But he heard a rattling of pans in the galley and looked in, grinning. Wo Fong took one glance at his uniform, scowled, and then turned away. As the clatter grew louder Caleb's grin faded and he headed for the poop deck. He found the skipper in the chart house, holding a cup of coffee to his lips. But the sipping stopped at once. The captain's fingers tapped on the cup while he studied the newly made drummer boy from top to bottom. "My stars, how sad!" he muttered to himself, and slowly shook his head. He took a deep breath, then suddenly stood up.

"I've written to your parents," he said crisply before he went out. "And my very last order to you is that you write one yourself here and now!"

Caleb sat down, took up the captain's quill, and dipped it into the inkwell. As he spoke to his parents on paper and saw their faces before him, he couldn't help wondering if he'd made a terrible mistake. He finished the letter, put it in an envelope, addressed it, and got up.

Now he went to the sick bay. Duval lay on his back with his eyes closed. His dark skin had turned grey. And if he was only sleeping, then why was his chest so still?

Kneeling beside the bed, Caleb poked him gently. There was no movement, and Caleb felt his own heart thump. Fearful now, he shook him again.

The eyelids slowly lifted. They studied his uniform, then rested kindly on his face. Caleb felt he needn't say anything. His friend understood.

When Duval licked his lips, Caleb brought him a cup of water. "I want you to listen to me," Duval murmured, forcing himself to lift his head. "If you ever are down there alone and can't get back on your own, look for my people to help you."

Weak as Duval was, he pressed Caleb's arm until it hurt. "Find some black man or woman who will meet your eyes without turning away or staring down at the ground. Tell this person that you have a friend in the north who a long time ago followed the Drinking Gourd."

"The Drinking Gourd?"

"They will understand that it means freedom. May God protect you and guide you to Jonathan, Caleb. You *are* your brother's keeper." Duval sank back exhausted and closed his eyes. Caleb went out.

The captain, who had been pacing the poop deck, stopped to shake hands and wish him well. Wo Fong was waiting on the main deck near the top of the rope ladder. "Foolish youth, take this."

"What's inside?"

"Are you asking what a cook would put in a bag?"

Caleb brightened at once, but then he turned serious. "Mr. Duval seems so weak. Will he be all right?"

"Yes and no," answered Wo Fong. "Until there is real freedom, he will never be all right."

Caleb was on his way out of the yard when he met Joshua Gooden coming in. The man's slight limp had become more of a weave, and there was a hint of rum on his breath. "Well, I'm a bosun again, or I will be if ever the ship leaves harbor!" he said, and began to look the boy over. He seemed to sober up at once. "Had to do it, eh?"

Caleb nodded.

"Well then, there's something I want you to take with you wherever you go," said Gooden, dipping into a pocket. "Because you can march forever, but you'll never slosh the sea water out of you."

He drew out a seashell and pressed it into the boy's hand. "There's going to come a time when you'll look all around you and see nothing but land and land and land. Your heart's going to long for the shore and the sound of the waves—and that's when you put this to your ear. You'll hear that roar, and it will bring you peace."

Caleb thanked him and walked on, gulping hard. For the second time in his life, he felt as if he was leaving home.

7

Caleb returned to the drill field still in time to bed down in a round tent with a dozen other drummer boys. They all lay on mats with their feet in the center, like the spokes of a wheel. Some of those feet stank so badly that he ran his hand along the canvas of the tent until he found a rip then shoved his nose up against the hole. Sleep came at last, but it was still dark outside when a bugle call sounded reveille.

The boys got up yawning, groggy, and rubbing their eyes. Some of them had been in the Drum Corps for a week or more and already knew enough to have gone to bed with their uniforms on. There was nothing for them to do but shove in their shirttails and shove into their shoes—yet even they weren't quick enough for the one-armed sergeant.

He stuck his head in howling, "What's the matter with you in here? You think this man's war is going to wait for you? Roll call! On the double! Fall out!"

They scrambled from the tent, still throwing on their uniforms. But a little corporal waiting for them boomed, "Did he say come out naked?" Dashing back, they threw

the straps of their drums over their necks and piled out
again to line up side by side.

The corporal held a board with a roster sheet on it,
and while the sergeant paced up and down in front of
them, he barked their names.

"Ames!"

"Here!

"Bartlett!"

"Here!"

He yelled out several others, but when he came to
"Strong," no one spoke up. "STRONG!" the corporal
roared again.

Before the half-awake Caleb could remind himself who
that was, the sergeant had raced over to plant a big nose
up against his. "Forgot your name *already,* dummy?"

Caleb's face jerked back, the sergeant's spit all over
it. "No it's . . . it's Strong! William Strong."

"Uh-huh. Then answer to it!"

"Here!"

The sergeant backed away.

"What's it really?" whispered the boy to his left when
the roll call went on. "Don't worry, most of us lied,
too."

"Peasley."

"Peasley," snickered the drummer on his right.
"Sounds like something small and green that you eat."

When several boys laughed aloud, the sergeant whirled
around, waving his stump. "This war ain't no joke. And
any of you who'll take a walk down to the nearest hospital will find that out soon enough."

"But these is only *boys,* Sergeant," sneered the corporal, at the same time rolling a ball of chewing tobacco
from one cheek to another. "And you know how boys

84

is. Why they think each of them sure as punch is gonna live forever!''

"That so?" the sergeant said, kicking a patch of mud off the toe of his shoe. "Well, maybe they ought to ask themselves how come the army is all the time signing up new drummers."

"A right fine idea, Sergeant. 'Cause maybe these boys figure all they'll ever have to do is just keep tapping out them camp calls we've been learning 'em. Why sure, and marching troops all around some other drill field. They don't know yet how that's all gonna change the very first time any Johnny Reb catches sight of them."

"Yes, well Johnny Reb, boys," said the sergeant, "that there's a feller who has growed up shootin' at moving targets—deer an' bear an' possum. He's got a musket now that's become turned into a rifle, which can put a hole through your drum and into you at half a mile. He's got artillery backing him up that you can't even see before shot and shell comes pouring down out of the sky right straight at you! All you boys is replacements for the drummers what's already dead or wounded! Why? On account of there ain't no such thing as staying out of a fight! Not especially when that grey line comes charging down at you with fixed bayonets. That's when you'd best know how to defend yourselves."

The sergeant paused to hook his only thumb under his belt and hitch up his pants. His eyes roved over their stunned faces. "Hear my words good, boys," he began again slowly. "When that enemy comes swooping on down some hill, you ain't gonna be one bit different from infantry no matter what you signed up for. Don't count on Johnny Reb letting you live just 'cause you're holding some drum 'stead of a gun. He ain't likely to be much older'n what you are. And he ain't taking no chances on leaving somebody behind him.''

The corporal gave a little cough and the sergeant turned to him. "You wanted to say something else, Corporal Smith?''

"No, I just wanted to spit," said the corporal.

"Watch him do it, boys," said the sergeant while the corporal shot out a long stream of tobacco juice. "Because that there spit is more'n any drummer boy's life is going to be worth if he ain't already learned how to take care of hisself when the fighting starts.''

"Now, that is a fact, boys," chimed in the corporal, wiping his mouth on his sleeve. "And Sergeant Tykes here may have only one arm, but there ain't nobody better than he is at teaching real soldiering. There is only one real big problem, though . . . which is the law.''

"Y'see boys," the sergeant started to say, but the corporal gave another little cough and rolled his eyes sideways. An officer was passing nearby on his way to the encampment on the other side of the drill field. They waited until he was gone. The boys waited, too. It was as if everyone now was part of a little conspiracy.

"According to regulations, boys," the sergeant began again in a low and much friendlier voice, "you are not supposed to git any guns and bayonets. That's because, even with all your lying 'bout how old you are, you ain't the right age to be real soldiers yet. And if any of them tenderhearted ladies who come to watch with the major at dress parade found out you was being trained for fighting, why that would mean our heads—the corporal's and mine. Which is a chance we couldn't take.''

"So boys," put in the corporal, starting to crack his knuckles, "it comes down to you havin' three choices here. The first is we don't learn you nothin' 'bout guns at all. The second is we do learn you the three firing positions, but only using sticks 'stead of muskets. You don't shoot at no targets. You don't get to learn nothing 'bout usin' the ramrod to load the cartridge down the muzzle, stuff like that.''

He paused while the drummers threw quick and worried glances at each other. Caleb thought he already knew what was coming. Still, he, too, waited breathlessly.

"And the third is," said the sergeant slowly, "I find us a supply of Enfield rifles."

"That's because them Springfields are too heavy for most of you," the corporal put in helpfully.

"Now, some of you already know," resumed the sergeant, "that daytimes I do double duty down at a recruiting station. But after you boys drum out taps for the camp, why, real quiet like we'll all sneak off yonder a couple of miles into the woods. Then you boys kin learn some target shooting."

"Also," put in the corporal, "cleanin' and takin' care of that piece of equipment so it don't blow up on you in your face."

"Right you are," declared the sergeant, taking over again. "Also what kinds o' heavy fire to listen for when you're gettin' close to the seat of battle, and when to start duckin' for a ditch or usin' your mess pan right quick to dig some kind of a hole to lie flat in."

The corporal nodded. "And how to watch out for them iron minnie balls when they come bouncing and skippin' over the ground straight at you. Plus other little things, like flying slices o'metal that'll go right through you. It all adds up, boys, to staying alive long enough to see your mothers again."

Caleb, like the others, had gone a bit pale. Still in all, he'd been to enough country fairs back home to know a sales pitch when he heard one. The sergeant settled back on his heels and began to talk about money.

"Now, my question, boys, is this. If the corporal and me is willin' to take this risk for you, what are you going to do for us? Now you is all drawin' soldiers' pay, just like any man—thirteen dollars a month. There is better ways to spend it right now than going down to the sutler's wagon and buying sweet things to eat. I want you boys to think on that when you go off to eat. But keep it to yourselves. Understand? Now, are there any questions?"

"If we're not supposed to have any muskets," said a confused drummer, "then how can we take them with us when we get sent out to our regiments?"

"Well, you kaint. These'll be loans, boys. Just fer practice, is all. That's the best we kin do."

"But then how do we get them when we need them?"

"Oh, that." The sergeant grinned. "That won't be no problem at all out there in the war. First regular soldier that drops dead near you, why you just pick up his."

Sales pitch or not, this was real enough to shoot an icy feeling though Caleb's stomach.

"Right face!" bawled the corporal.

Watching how the boy next to him did it, Caleb's right foot swung on the heel before the left foot moved up to join it.

"Mark time. March!"

"I hate this army!" someone muttered under his breath.

"Who don't?" barked the corporal, overhearing. "But

88

you're all too late, boys, too late by a damn sight! *Forward march!*"

The mess hall was a big wooden shed on the far side of the drill field. To get there, they had to pass rows of tents the shape of Indian wigwams. These were for men who had recovered from wounds and were waiting to be sent back to their regular regiments. There seemed to be no officer around to give them orders. Some of these men were walking ahead of the boys toward the huge kettles where the cooks stood with their ladles. But others, Caleb noticed, had started cooking fires of their own in front of the tents.

"Watch out for little friends in them peas and beans," one of the fire tenders warned as the drummers filed past. "And that coffee will kill a mule."

On the floor inside another tent, several men were starting to play cards. Not one of them was in uniform. Caleb saw city jeans with suspenders, farmer's overalls, and even a couple of men in white straw summer hats. He noticed a whiskey bottle being passed.

Leaning against a tent pole watching them, a man called out, "Hey, Sarge, these fleecy little lambs you got here—have you clipped all their pay off yet for your retirement?"

"You mind what you say," the sergeant sneered back. "Don't somebody got to learn 'em how to stay alive?"

"Stay alive for what?" grunted another man, with a skillet in his hand, frying bacon. "So they can keep being sent, like us, back into hell?"

"Don't be so scared, little rabbit," snapped the corporal. "Ain't nobody dumb enough to send you back."

"I took three slams of canister in the gut, and I'm still

walking!'' cried the man, throwing his skillet down. ''Who you callin' names?''

''Him and me is!'' cried the sergeant. ''And just me alone, I can whip your hide with one stump tied behind my back.''

With these insults flying, angry-looking men began to pour out of tents. ''Tap us out the mess call, boys,'' said the corporal quickly, to head off being outnumbered in a fight. ''Lemme hear it.'' And he began to chant as they drummed:

> ''Soupy, soupy, soupy, without any bean
> Porky, porky, porky, without any lean
> Coffee, coffee, coffee, without any cream!''

The boys kept it up until they reached the food line. Shifting his drum to the side, Caleb took his tin cup and plate and followed the other drummers to the long mess hall table that had been set aside for them. ''How much you think we're gonna be charged?'' they started asking each other as soon as they sat down.

Caleb shrugged. ''Why don't we all say we'll pay half, and see how that goes?''

''Sounds fair,'' a boy said. ''But what if they want everything we get? Seems to me, we'd have to go along with it.''

''Maybe,'' replied Caleb. ''But back where I come from, the fishermen stick together on a price. If they didn't, the dealers would buy their catch for almost nothing.''

Though he'd spoken up, Caleb's heart wasn't really in this conversation. He started to pick up on what else was going on in the mess hall.

Faces were edgy, and although nobody was shouting, the place seemed on the edge of exploding. At a table nearby, one of the men was speaking to nobody in particular. "I just read in the paper that the President's going to change the commanding general again. Anybody recall how many that is now?"

"Four so far in one year!" snorted a soldier at a different table. "And not one of them fit to hold the bridle on Robert E. Lee's horse."

"You sound like you joined the wrong army, friend," called a voice from somewhere in the middle of the hall.

"No, but it sure looks as if all the good officers joined the wrong army!"

"Not all of 'em!" A young man yelled, climbing up on his bench. "There's General Ulysses S. Grant. And if we could just bring him east from the Mississippi to the Potomac, we could actually *win* for a change!"

"Or maybe Grant knows better than to waste his time trying to lead the Army of the Potomac," grumbled one of the men.

Dead silence fell at once over the mess hall. Not a tin plate or cup clinked against a table. Every eye turned towards the soldier who had said those words.

"I . . . I didn't mean it. Look, I'm sorry," he stammered, beginning to shrivel.

"I don't have any wine, but I make this toast," shouted one of the men, jumping to his feet. He lifted his coffee mug in the air. "To the men who never give up. Who never stop fighting back. Who never stop believing in America. The Army of the Potomac!"

Then they all stood. "To the Army of the Potomac!" shouted every voice in the room, including Caleb's.

"I am glad to see there is spirit here!" boomed a

powerful voice. And as everyone snapped to attention the major commanding the camp took long, quick strides to the center. "Men, this evening will be spit and polish all the way. This place will shine, every tent will be in order, and each of you will be in full uniform. I have just gotten word that we are to be visited at dress parade by the President of the United States. There is much to do. Finish eating quickly and get started."

For the rest of that day the drummers, fife players, and the buglers practiced without stop. At first an old music master from Germany tried to get them all to play "Hail to the Chief" together, but he gave up in disgust. Next, since the President had been born in Kentucky, he tried to have them do "My Old Kentucky Home." But that sounded even worse. Finally, with the fife players standing on either side and the drummers in the middle, they were lined up at the edge of the field, more or less ready with "Yankee Doodle."

First came a squadron of cavalry. Then a coach and four horses arrived and came to a stop. The door was opened from the outside by an officer—and Abraham Lincoln stepped out in a long black coat and a very high black hat, the shape of a stovepipe.

The music master waved his arm to begin, but not a drumstick thumped, not a fifer piped. Boys watched in dumbstruck awe as the eyes of the tall man whom millions called Father Abraham looked at *them*. To Caleb, it seemed as if the President was like one of those long, thin pines in Maine that had been trimmed of their branches to go into ships. This tree stood upright until the shoulders, where they were just a little bit rounded, as if the President was carrying behind him a soldier's knapsack of his own. When the music master, tapping his baton with rage, tried to get their attention again, Mr. Lincoln gently held up his hand, as if to say it was all right to remain still.

Caleb began to feel very sorry for this man who now went by them in silence. The President walked past the color guard who was holding the flag, and he climbed the steps to the little platform. Then he took off his hat and glanced over the field.

"It is sometimes said to me," he began in a voice that was soft and strong at the same time, "that it isn't a very dignified thing for the President of the United States of America to make jokes in serious times."

A thin smile began to play across his face, and he went on. "But then, what is a feller supposed to do when one thing reminds him of something else? Now this Army of the Potomac puts me in mind today of the only mule I ever heard of that once began to talk. That unusual critter was hunkered down in front of a wooden bridge that he just did not want to step foot on. The mule skinner who owned him had been pulling at him and pushing him and whacking him with a log and yelling all manner of cusswords at him. This went on till finally that mule decided it was about time to speak up for himself:

" 'Now I don't mean any disrespect to you, sir,' he said. 'But the two of us have got to put this here matter straight. It used to be that I didn't have anything against crossing bridges whenever I come to them. In fact, I looked forward to it. But the last time you drove me onto one, it like to broke right under me. I fell head over hoof into the river and saved myself from being drowned by the skin of my teeth. Now, sir, if that had happened only once, I'd say anybody can make a mistake. But there has been one falling down bridge after another. So here we

93

are again. And I ain't about to refuse orders exactly, but I do have a little request. Would you please mind going ahead of me and jumping up and down on it real hard till I say stop?' ''

Caleb heard a chuckle here and there, but no one really laughed, and Mr. Lincoln's voice turned sad. "Very soon you men who were already wounded will go back to your regiments to fight again. I would be obliged if you'd bring this message to your comrades from Old Abe. Tell them I know that they deserve better. Tell them that this is one mule skinner who would gladly, and with all his heart, step out on that next bridge first. But the plain truth is that I can send nothing ahead of them but my prayers and those of a grateful nation. Tell them that when at last they do find a bridge that holds, they will carry across it the whole of the United States of America. May God protect the fighting men of the only country I can think of that was ever born in Freedom.''

That evening Caleb went to the sergeant's tent and found him pulling a cork out of a bottle with his teeth.

"Where are the rest of the boys, Strong?"

"They sent me."

The sergeant offered the bottle, but Caleb shook his head. "Well, then, what'll it be?"

Caleb had intended to bargain—but somehow he just couldn't get the words started. Now he surprised himself by blurting, "We're not going to pay for it, Sergeant."

"What's that? Why not?"

The sergeant's face had turned mean, but Caleb stiffened. "Because if what you told us about how it will be during the fighting is true—"

"It is."

"Then we've got a right to be trained."

"Maybe. But I don't have to do it."

"I guess not, if you don't think so," said Caleb, starting to leave. "But I thought you were our sergeant."

"Come back here, Private!"

Caleb turned around.

The sergeant's eyes narrowed and his voice grew threatening. "If you're going to tell tales to the captain on me . . ."

"I'm not."

"Wouldn't do you no good if you was. Everyone makes money on the side around here."

"All I know is somebody else's got to make a deal with you. I won't." He was trembling—but with anger, not fear. "Can I go now, Sergeant?"

"There's something about you . . ." The sergeant peered at him more closely. "You seen the elephant already?"

"What's that?"

"Been under fire?"

"Yes, I've seen the elephant," said Caleb quietly.

"Where?"

"Board ship."

"Then what are you doing here?"

"Got to go down to Fredericksburg, find my missing brother."

The sergeant tilted his head back to take another swig from the bottle. But he found himself staring hard at the boy instead. "That battlefield's thirty miles or more from where our regiments in Virginia are right now. It's behind enemy lines. And the way things are going now, we ain't likely to ever get there."

"I will," said Caleb.

"All by yourself?"

"If I have to."

"Now, lookee here." The sergeant stood up. "I might think 'bout doin' it on the free. But the corporal, he always needs something extra to spend on the ladies."

"Not from me."

The sergeant took a long breath while he thought the matter over. "You wrote out that enlistment paper by yourself, so I know you had schooling. Right?"

"Some."

"How are you at writing letters?"

"Not too good," mumbled the boy, thinking of his parents. But he'd misunderstood why the question was asked.

"Got to be better than me, now that my writing hand's been shot off. I can fill out a form with the other one, but that's about it. You wouldn't think you was paying me a bribe if I asked you to write for me to my wife, would you?"

"No, I guess not."

The sergeant tapped on his bottle. "And you wouldn't talk about what goes in it? Not to anyone?"

"No, I wouldn't."

"All right, then I'll take a chance on you. Pen's on the table. Paper and jar of ink's in the box under my cot."

When the boy was ready, he began to dictate, "Dearest Mildred. Weather is fine. I am in good health. I am sorry that I ain't got around to answering your letters and that it set you to wondering if I've been getting them. Yes, I have, and I've been reading them, too. And they are mighty fine letters at that—which I thank you kindly for—telling me about you and about the farm and about the children. Only I just didn't know how to pass on the news that when your husband comes home, he'll be a cripple. Hardly good to do nothing . . .''

Caleb looked up. ''In my family it wouldn't matter to us if my brother lost some part of his body, just as long as he was alive . . .''

''That right?'' said the sergeant, turning away so that he wouldn't be seen wiping his eyes. ''Well, we'll see.''

After that, the boys did get for free some weapons and survival training. It was only in secret and on their own time, of course—after endless hours of practicing their drum calls on the march. With very few minutes left over to sit around and relax and no way to keep their eyes open anyhow, they flopped on their cots to sleep like the dead.

It was in the middle of the night several weeks later that Caleb was quietly but firmly shaken awake by the sergeant. He got up in a daze, dressed quickly in spite of it, and followed him out of the tent. The sergeant waved his stump at the distant road where men were marching four abreast in a silent line that went all the way back into the darkness.

''That regiment you asked to be sent to? That's it, down on the road. For some reason or other it's moving out way ahead of time. Slipping out is more like it. Better grab your drum and hop down there.''

Caleb was confused. ''The column's heading the wrong way, isn't it, to set out for Virginia? North, instead of down to the docks?''

The sergeant scratched his head. ''See what you mean, and I can't figure it out. Some kind of special mission must have come up. I know why you wanted so bad to go down to Virginia, but it's too late to change your mind now, Billy. This here order is already cut. Here, give it to an officer. And good luck.''

Caleb ducked back into the tent for his drum, and when he came out again, the sergeant hadn't moved from the spot. He grabbed Caleb by the arm, pressing hard. "I want you to remember what I taught you. First man who dies, you grab his musket and cartridges—and bayonet, too, if it ain't fixed on yet. Then you fight like hell to stay alive. That's the one part of the war every soldier goes through by himself."

When Caleb ran down to the end of the road, he found a major on horseback and handed up his orders. The officer glanced at the paper, and quietly returned it, saying, "Tell the captain of G Company, it's the next one back, that I said to take you in line. We are not giving marching drumbeats, though, until we're out of the city. No music, no singing. We don't have to advertise ourselves to spies."

Several hours later an order was given to halt, then to form the lines of a square that was hollow inside. As the men stood staring at each other across a field of growing corn their colonel rode into the center. He was small and had a nose like a beak—and to Caleb, it seemed as if a crow was perched on that snow-white horse.

From under the beak a thin voice screeched, "Men of the Sixth Washington! This may be the darkest moment of the war! Robert E. Lee has invaded the North with all his forces. His regiments have slipped past our army and left it behind in Virginia. Think of it, the enemy is on the loose somewhere here in the state of Maryland. He's heading for Pennsylvania with no one in front of him to stop him. That will be our job! Find Lee. Cut him off. Dig in and hold him long enough for our own forces to catch up. You will now understand why we must march day and night until we close with the enemy in battle. Soldiers, rejoice in your hearts. This is a task worthy of heroes!''

Caleb's eyes were far from the only ones that watched without blinking as the colonel prodded his horse into a bouncy trot and rode out of the square. Standing barely two feet from the captain and the lieutenant of G Company, he could overhear their furious whispers.

"But this is suicide, Captain! How can headquarters be sending a thousand troops against an army of eighty thousand?"

"Because that idiot of a glory hound talked them into it! No big sacrifice for them if it should count for nothing. We're green troops, anyway."

"At least he could have asked for a couple more regiments to back us up."

"But the colonel wouldn't, don't you see? Then they'd put a general in charge!"

An order was shouted, and the regiment went back into marching formation. The bugles sounded. Caleb, like the boys in the other companies, began to roll his drum. "Well, I sure asked for it!" he told himself, his own heart thumping as loudly in his ears as the drum.

The men behind him and in the other companies struck up a marching song. At first their voices were shaky, but then they grew stronger, and stronger still.

"The Union forever! Hurray, boys, hurrah!
Down with the traitors, up with the stars
While we rally round the flag boys, rally once again
Shouting the battle cry of FREEDOM!''

8

They were deep into the countryside and the last of many songs had died out long ago. The soldiers no longer marched in step. For twenty straight hours they'd been trudging across wheat fields and through woods. No stopping to rest or to eat—and the steamy heat made the end of June seem like the middle of summer. The men sweated till their clothes stank, their socks rubbed away, and their heels blistered. Their backpacks felt heavier with each mile. And long after night fall came, they were deep into brambly bushes, tripping over their feet, tearing their skin on thorns.

Though there were grown men all around him, Caleb held up with the best of them. He was strong for his age and used to working long burning-hot days in an open boat. And though he'd never done much of it on his feet, all the marching he'd been put through while training to become a drummer had made up for that. Still an uneasy feeling had been building in him, the longer the regiment kept heading inland. This was farther away from seashore than he had ever been. Without realizing it, he began to lift his nose to each breeze for the scent of salt water.

And more than once, when that failed, he reached edgily for the seashell in his pocket. Being surrounded by so much land was making a fisherman's son feel closed in.

"Fall out!"

The order came as the men staggered free of the brambles and out onto a field. They dropped their packs and dived headfirst into the high grass. Some rolled over on their sides and were instantly asleep. But others had gone sprawling into wild strawberries. Sweet smelling and juicy, they were so close that a fellow barely had to flick his tongue to snap one up . . .

Once started who could stop? Next thing a fellow knew he was up on his hands and knees to scurry in the starlight for more. By then, how could anyone, especially Caleb, stay serious while scrambling about on all fours, cramming his mouth? In a few gulps hundreds of men became armed berry throwers—and the great sticky fight was on! Schoolboy laughter rang out . . .

And that brought the colonel from his newly pitched tent. "Since you're all so full of high spirits," he proclaimed, "there's no need to waste it on games. Saddle my horse! We're moving on."

Moaning, the men took up their packs and muskets. "Drummer," one of them said to Caleb, "if you ever beat taps for that officer's funeral, I'll be there whistling Dixie."

"Mind your tongue!" his lieutenant warned loudly. But under his breath he added, "I know how you feel, soldier."

"What's happening?" one of the few privates who'd been sleeping asked the friend whose foot had nudged him awake.

"Up and at 'em, Tom. We've been ordered out."

"Feels like I only fell asleep a minute ago," the woozy soldier declared.

"Nope, You've been deader'n a log for hours."

"You wouldn't be joshing me, would ye?" the first private asked woozily as he sat up, reaching for his backpack . . . .

"Would I pitch you a wrong ball, farm boy?"

"Then how come I'm so tuckered out?"

"Beats me," said the second private, shouldering his musket. "Must be old age."

"Old, huh?" A big grin opened across the first private's face. "This reminds me. We got some celebrating coming to us a week from Sunday. That's my birthday."

"God and the colonel willing, we'll still be around by then," his friend remarked glumly.

"Bad luck to think like that," Caleb put in quickly when the first private's grin started to freeze on his face.

"You *hear* what he said? The drummer boy's right! I won't go putting my mind onto it that way. And don't you go doing it, neither." The smile returned, and he beamed it at Caleb.

The next day was worse than the first for these weary men. The sun came up already blazing like a furnace. They were on open ground now, with hardly a shade tree in sight. Before morning was half done with, three men dazed by sunstroke went wandering off in confusion until they fell to their knees. The regiment had only one horse-drawn ambulance, so there was not nearly enough room to pick up all those who collapsed. The rest were dragged into bushes and told to rest until evening, then try to catch up as best they could.

Meanwhile, there was still the afternoon to go. And this was even worse because now the sun was no longer beating down on their backs. Its furious, slanting rays burned into the left side of their faces. Some shifted their caps to block it, but this left parts of their heads uncovered, and now the sun was getting in front of them. Other men ripped weeds out of the ground by the roots and plastered them over their burning skin.

When they drew near at last to a wide, fast flowing stream, nobody waited to find out what the colonel wanted or didn't want. Dropping muskets, packs, and at least one drum, they became a wildly charging herd.

Nobody was faster than Caleb. Darting past others, he was out on a jutting rock in no time, peering down into water deep enough for a leap in all his clothes. It was during the split second when he was still falling through air that he heard the muffled snort of a horse. The first bullets from the other side of the stream crashed past him into other men just then dashing into the stream.

Bullets pinged the water above him. And one, weaving under the surface like a fish, nipped his left cheek. He barely felt the hot bite, but a trail of blood flowed away from it. This flowed into a thicker and widening circle of red as a floating dead man turned over just above him. Caleb looked into the face of a farm boy who would never celebrate this birthday come Sunday and a week.

Horror and panic seized him by the throat. He only knew that he had to get to safety! Frantically he tore away his shoes. His legs drew under to kick out like a turtle. His arms made angel wings in the water. The screams, the shots, the deaths would stay in another world if only he could keep moving away! If only he could keep holding his breath. If only no bullets turned into fish again!

But shouldn't he go up and grab that dead man's musket and fight? What he was doing now, wasn't that running away just like that coward, his bro—He caught himself. It was to stop a thought just like this one that had made Caleb spring upon Shiprat a million years ago! And he burst to the surface through bodies of dead men.

There was return fire now. Soldiers still on shore lay on their stomachs desperately shooting at targets on the opposite shore they could not see. Others were falling back to a line of bushes, jamming new cartridges down the muzzles of their weapons and firing as they went. But there was little cover anywhere. They were hit where they lay, or they crashed to the ground while the enemy kept firing without reloading! From behind their rocks and the bushes piled on top for disguise, these marksmen were using the repeater rifles that only cavalry men had.

If it had not been for the colonel's galloping white horse, Caleb might have been spotted and shot dead straight away. It sprang out of the bushes, with the colonel on it, pointing his sword at the stream, yelling *"Charge!"*

A hail of bullets crashed into the water just ahead of him. His terror-struck horse stopped dead on the shore and reared up on its hind legs, while the front ones kicked at empty air. The colonel tugged hard at the reins, which was the wrong thing to do. The animal toppled over backward. Half a ton of quivering flesh crashed to the ground, with the colonel underneath.

Only a few in the regiment had started to follow their commanding officer. The charge broke off before it began, and from the enemy shore Caleb heard the cry "Cease fire!"

Rebel marksmen stood up from behind their rocks. The Union men who were still able to fight lowered their guns. Those who'd been wounded on the ground sat up if they could. Those still in the river, who like Caleb had stayed alive, crawled out and sat down.

Dazedly, these survivors watched a line of horsemen in gray uniforms come down to the water's edge and spread out along it. They held their carbines upright on their knees. Not one of them showed a wound. And they seemed ready at a word to spring back into action.

On a rocky ledge above these hard-eyed fighters, two mounted officers appeared. One carried the Confederate flag in his right hand. On the collar of the other, stars flashed in the sunlight. And Caleb, for a moment, thought he was staring at Robert E. Lee.

But General Lee's hair, as everyone knew, was snow-white. This was a fierce-looking red-bearded general with feathers sprouting from a side of his hat. "I give the rest of you your lives, Yanks!" he boomed out. "Go back to Washington. Tell Mr. Lincoln that Jeb Stuart sends his regards. And we'll come for him when we're ready!"

With a wave of his hand the leader of General Lee's cavalry turned his men away from the river and rode off.

Caleb ambled back to the rock where he had jumped in and squatted down beside his drum. A bullet had gone in one side and out the other. He tested the skin with his knuckles and heard a sound. He supposed that was good, but his thoughts were coming very slowly and he forgot the one he'd just had. The next one was to look down through the water for his shoes. When a body floated by, he looked away. Now he tried to stand up, but that made him feel dizzy.

Someone was talking to him. He looked up. The major who'd first let him into the regiment was leaning over him. "Drummer, let's see that graze," he said, and examined Caleb's face.

"Well, it's not too bad, but keep this side tied up to slow the bleeding. You don't want to lose too much or you'll pass out. The surgeon is working over by the medical supply wagon. Go over there and give him a little time to get to you. Tell him I said it needs stitching. You'll be all right."

"I . . . I tried to run away, sir," Caleb heard himself mumble miserably as the major turned to go.

The major stopped. "That's exactly what a drummer is *supposed* to do."

Caleb wanted to accept this, but couldn't. He shook his head bitterly. Sure, maybe some other drummer boy was!

"Well, son," sighed the major, "if you want to take a share in the blame, there's plenty to go around. If we officers had controlled our men, they wouldn't have been sitting ducks. If the colonel had sent scouts out ahead of the regiment, we might have been warned of the ambush. If, if, if. As for the men, they mostly tried to save themselves, as you did. And it was pretty much too late to do anything else. Well, this command is mine now, so I have to go pull it together."

The major's words brought Caleb out of his funk. He saw now that there was work going on. And laying down his drum, he joined in. With others he hauled men to the shore, bringing the dead to one grassy place, the wounded to another. When the last of these had been carried off by the medics, he grabbed a flat slab of rock and became one of the grave diggers. Though grisly, the hard work helped him. Here was something that he *could* do!

He was settling one of the corpses into a shallow hole when the soldier doing it with him said, "You ain't got no shoes. Take his."

"Couldn't do that."

106

"Don't be stupid," snapped the man. "What's *he* going to do with them? Go to a dance?"

Without answering, Caleb started brushing dirt over the body. But the soldier fell to his knees and yanked off the shoes. "Do like I tell you!" He burst into tears. "They're my *brother's!*"

There was nothing the boy could do but thank him. Caleb was lacing them on when he fainted. It was the sting of a metal point going into his cheek that brought him back, jerking his head.

"Hold still, boy, so I can sew this."

Caleb's eyelids snapped up. He was lying among the wounded on a muddy patch of ground near the medical wagon. A medic squatted beside him with a threaded sewing needle that was caked with blood. Blood that looked already dry. "That's not mine is it?" he demanded wildly, thinking of Wo Fong and what he would have said about this.

"What's the difference?"

Caleb sprang to his feet. "Well, if you don't know, then let me be!"

The medic seemed to think that he had a crazy patient on his hands. "All right, I'll wipe it off," he said quietly, and rubbed the needle on his sleeve. "There."

But Caleb hurried away to where the stream was flowing clear and lowered his torn cheek into it. The flow of his blood thinned to a trickle, then stopped. Rolling onto his back, he lay there watching geese fly overhead. They made him think of seabird, which brought an ache to his heart. He took the shell from his pocket, put it to his ear, and listened to the roar.

The major spoke to him again. "You don't belong in the army, son."

107

Caleb hastily scrambled to his feet. "Yes, I do, sir!"

"No, you belong at home, in school, like my own children. I never believed in allowing drummer boys into the service. And we have just," he sighed heavily, "put two of them in the ground. I refuse having to write to your family as well. The regiment—what's left of it—is pushing on. The wounded are heading back. So are you."

"Please, don't do that, sir!"

"I am. That's an order." Now he called out, "This one goes!

"Yes, sir!" A limping corporal used the hickory cane he'd taken from a medic to point at a line forming behind the ambulance.

Caleb took an arm of a man with a leg wound. Behind him the soldiers who could still fight were forming up, too, awaiting orders to move out. From somewhere upstream an officer called back news of a place shallow enough to wade across without soaking the guns.

Caleb left with the wounded, feeling that there was no one with less reason than he to be taking this journey back to safety. What, he asked himself, was a torn little flap of skin? Nothing! The farther he moved from the men still ready to fight, the hotter burned his shame. This was all wrong!

Slowly, and with many pauses to rest, the wounded moved on in the gathering twilight. The corporal would limp back to cheer the others. The first farm they came to, he promised, the animals would be kicked out of the barn and everyone would have a bed of hay to rest upon. Caleb didn't wait for that to happen before he broke away.

If he was going to overtake the regiment, he'd have to put on speed. His pack and blanket dropped away as he ran. The drum was light and necessary. As long as he had that, no one could tell him that he didn't belong. He did belong, and somehow he would prove that to the major! Prove it to everyone!

He flitted through dark woods where the tree shadows left pools of blackness on the ground. Roots tripped and slowed him, and there was a constant shortage of breath that hurt his chest. But he would not allow himself to stop until he reached the stream. He'd been listening for the gurgling splash of the water. Yet somehow there was nothing until he'd broken out into the open. And then he was suddenly in the presence of the newly dead.

He reminded himself that he wanted a musket. But the only ones he could find here were stuck into the ground as markers for the graves—sacred to the dead! Leaving them be, he went looking for the shallow place where the rest of the regiment must have waded across.

He found it. And on the far side, he saw a musket that had come to rest among the reeds. If it had been ruined by the soaking, he had no idea. Nor was there a box of cartridges to go along with it. Still he took it and went on.

The woods here weren't more than a few miles deep. Afterward came rolling land that had been cleared for raising crops and for pasturing herds of milk cows. The night was bright enough to spot a soldier's cap that had fallen here and a chewing tobacco wrapper tossed there. And whenever these signs failed him, Caleb drew a line from the Drinking Gourd to the North Star. The regiment was heading west by north. Catching up should be easy for a fellow who knew how to steer by the stars.

9

Caleb never found the regiment exactly. Hunger brought him to a farmer's door the next morning. He was still knocking on it when the barrel of a shotgun went into the small of his back.

"This is a Union home and all my menfolk are off fighting for it," a woman said gruffly. "But last night I had half my chickens stolen by defenders of the Republic. Day before that, the other half. And all my sides of ham were taken by rebel boys, who at least were polite. You buying or robbing?"

"Buying!"

"Five cents for milk. Five cents for pie. Price may be high, but take it or leave it."

"I'll take it!"

"Put down your weapon—it's too big for you anyway—and come inside. Mind your manners with my daughter, but don't expect her to do the same. Are you a proper Christian?"

"Yes, ma'am." He propped his rifle against a wall and stepped away from it.

"What's your baptized name?" she asked, opening the door for him.

"Caleb."

As he went inside, a strawberry-haired girl peered at him over the rim of her knitting. "Ever had a day's worth of schooling, Caleb?"

"Of course."

"Of course? My! Maybe you're a scholar. And what exactly have you studied?"

Caleb stiffened up. "Oh, just about everything."

Her needles clicked away. She did not seem impressed. "Say something in Greek."

"E pluribus unum."

"That's Latin!"

"Just testing *you*," he said. "Can you tell me what it means?"

"*Pluribus* means too many. And *unum* means chickens. Too many chickens. Oh, my! Just look at your face!"

"I can't. I was born inside of it, looking out the other direction."

"You're lucky then. You won't have to see the scar that you're going to have unless Mama fixes it up."

"I'll do that right now," said the woman, with just the thinnest touch of a smile. "Then after I'm done, Melody can start picking on your table manners—and it'll be just as if her brothers hadn't gone off to the war."

Caleb spent a day in that house being teased and pampered until it felt like home. In the evening a neighbor came over to visit and share the news. He had returned that day from a small town named Hanover. On the way to it he'd seen rebel cavalrymen and their horses lying dead on the road, but no fighting. Then, while he was

111

busy about his business in Hanover, the town itself started filling up with Union regiments that had marched all the way from Virginia.

Mother and daughter gave a start. And out of the hush that followed, the girl asked in a choked voice, "Soldiers from around here, too?"

The farmer shook his head. He had asked around and couldn't find any Pennsylvania troops. But he did think there were more regiments in a town a few miles farther west. He'd heard the thud of cannon coming from the direction of Gettysburg.

Caleb had been sitting by the fire toasting his feet like Grandpa Peasley. Now he jumped up saying he had to leave right away. The women pleaded with him not to go. Hadn't he already been hurt and ordered to stay out of it? What, after all, did this tremendous war need one more drummer boy for? And why, at least, couldn't he stay the night to rest himself until he got back all his strength?

But when Caleb insisted on leaving, he found that his shoes had been hidden. "We'll strike this bargain, and no other," declared Melody's mother. "You wait until the morning milking, and I'll take you on the buckboard. You wouldn't get there any faster walking."

Caleb slept in the bed of one of Melody's brothers. Before dawn he was up again, leading the horse out so he could clean up the stall while she milked in the barn and threw seed to the chickens. The sun was just rising, very big and rosy, when her mother hitched the buckboard and told him to get in. Caleb started to mumble a sad goodbye, but Melody grabbed the harness and refused to let them ride off unless she went too. She got her way, and they all set off together along a dusty dirt road.

They ate fruit from a basket as they went along, and by and by Melody said, "I guess I made fun of you too much yesterday?"

"No, no. There's a person back home who does it all the time."

She gave him a sharp-eyed look. "*Person?* You mean a girl?"

"Yep."

As he reached for a peach, her hand closed around his wrist. "And what is she like?"

"Why, you won't find anyone smarter. Kind of tall and pretty, too. She's about twenty."

"Twenty! Why that's an old, old woman!"

"I'd mind it myself, except she's marrying my brother."

"Oh, your brother!"

Melody's mother smirked, and they all drove on. The grip on Caleb's hand had become a very light touch. Still, it made him uncomfortable—mostly because he'd started to notice she smelled like flowers.

Farther on, they came to a wider road that went off toward the west. And driving along it, they began to hear in the clear morning sky a sound like low thunder rolling down from the distance. Drawing closer to the town, they had to drive around the dead horses and bodies of rebel cavalrymen the neighbor had talked about.

"Serves them right!" Caleb cried aloud. "Johnny Reb's got back some of what he gave us!" But Melody gasped, drawing back her hand.

At once, he felt ashamed. What's wrong with me? he asked himself. What was happening in his brain? Death was death no matter who'd been killed.

"Both of you look away," he said.

The girl shook her head. "No! This is what my brothers have to see all the time. And it's what happened to my father."

"Well, in that case, there's something I'd better do here." Jumping down from the buckboard, he went back to the bodies and walked among them until he found one of those deadly repeating rifles and three bags of ammunition.

"They killed a lot of us with these," he explained, coming back with them.

When neither mother or daughter replied, he began to feel like a grave robber. "Look! We have to do these things." But the others only nodded. They drove on in silence. "All right! I'll throw the gun away!"

"Don't be stupid!" hissed Melody. And a moment or two later, she touched his hand again. It gave him a feeling of comfort that he wasn't sure he deserved.

At a burst of cannon fire louder than before, Melody's mother suddenly cried out, "Blueberries and huckleberries!" She pointed to a thick mesh of bushes along the road. "If nobody picks them in this heat, they'll dry up and die."

She made them all get out and start gathering. When the fruit basket was full, the women took off their bonnets. "Careful now. Don't do anything in a rush," she commanded. "If you crush any of these, the hat will be ruined!"

They were stalling him, of course. The berries could have been picked afterward, on the way back. Caleb knew this, yet he didn't say anything. How could he, when they were showing they cared?

At last they all started off again—and soon came to a crossroad where an army wagon had been set up to block the way. Behind it were columns of weary soldiers trudging along the other road. In between the men came horses pulling heavy cannons. The big farm horse hitched to the buckboard halted, sniffing the air as if it did not like being here. Caleb climbed down for the last time and thanked Melody and her mother for being so good to him.

As he watched the buckboard turn around, Melody called back over her shoulder, "If you don't write to us—" Her voice broke. "At least to say that you're alive—" Her voice broke again. She looked away for a moment, but now she darted him her most powerful frown yet. "I'll be very very angry with you!"

Caleb had a sudden wish to go after them. And why couldn't he do that if he wanted to? Hadn't that major practically shoved him out of the war anyway?

A voice barked at him. "Hey, you! What's your unit, and why ain't you with it?"

He started to mumble about an ambush scattering the Fifth Washington, but the provost guard was more interested in admiring his repeating rifle. "Stripped that off one of our own cavalry boys, did you?"

"No, off theirs."

"Yeah? Where do you think *Johnny Reb* got it? That's federal government issue. Maybe you better hand that over—considering you're just a drummer boy." He started to reach for the gun.

"This is mine! I'm keeping it." Before Caleb realized what he was doing, his fingers slid down to the trigger. That frightened him. He was scared of himself! Was this a bluff—or did he really mean it? He couldn't really shoot anyone, could he? At least, not over something like this!

The provost wasn't taking any chances. "All right. All

right. Fifth Washington, you say?'' He opened a little book and ran his finger down the pages. ''Well, it ain't showed up yet. But don't just hang around. Go report to some other outfit.''

''I, uh . . . I've got kin serving in the Twentieth Maine,'' Caleb said edgily. ''Can you tell me where I can find it?''

''That's one of the regiments in the Fifth Corps, ain't it?'' He leafed through his pad. ''Yep, it is. You missed Fifth Corps. Marched out to Gettysburg.''

''Where's that?''

''What? You can't guess?'' The provost gave a hard little laugh—and jerked a finger in the direction of the booming cannon. ''It's where the end of the world started yesterday. This column's going there, but it's slow as molasses. What you better do is forget about that road. Wait your chance to go cross it and get onto the foot trail on the other side. That way's a lot more direct on account of it's heading straight west. All right, there's a break coming up in the line. What are you waiting for! Get a move on.''

After hiking along for a few miles, Caleb came to a larger path that was being used by a mule train of supply wagons pulled by mules. A friendly drover waved him on to the back of one of the animals. It was a bumpy ride, but it sure beat walking, he thought, by a country mile!

He noticed after a while that the cannon fire had died down. Now, with his arms around the mule's neck, he listened to the *pop-pop-popping* of musket fire coming from somewhere farther on. The sound reminded him of Indian corn going off in a skillet at a county fair. For a while he could daydream about other things than men shooting at each other . . . and bodies falling.

116

When the mule splashed across a creek, he slipped off it at the other side and walked through an orchard. If there was supposed to be a town somewhere named Gettysburg, he sure couldn't see it. That place—and the fighting—must be on the other side of these hills, he thought. They were in a little valley behind rough-looking rises covered with trees. Those hills were strung together—and the line along their tops made a long ridge. There had been a lot of digging up there on Cemetery Ridge—tons of earth and rocks piled up for protection. Later that might give some protection from charging troops. Right now, those earthworks saved many a Union lad from some enemy marksman who could shoot a bird out of the sky—or even, it was said, the eye out of a bird.

Down at the bottom of the slope where Caleb was, were many other wagons and their animals. He saw big artillery pieces parked together, that had yet to be hauled up. There were men down here, too, who had not yet been thrown into the fight. Foot soldiers, off their feet at last, were sprawled out from exhaustion after their long and constant march from Virginia.

As he walked among them asking for the Twentieth Maine someone pointed to an area about a quarter of a mile farther down along the base of the ridge. He broke into a run, his heart leaping to see faces he recalled from Sunday Cove, Wiscasset, Pemaquid. Zigzagging past them, he hurried to the command tent. A captain stopped him outside of it demanding to know what he wanted.

Caleb swallowed hard. "I have to ask Colonel Chamberlain about my brother! Please! I've come all this way from Maine to find out!"

A tall man, his eyes still heavy from a catnap, came to the front to the tent. "Of whom are you speaking?"

For a moment Caleb was tongue-tied with fear of what this commanding officer would say about his brother. Through gritted teeth he said the name. "Lt. Jonathan Peasley."

"Peasley. Yes, I remember him. A fine officer. What do you want to know?"

Fine! The word exploded in his flabbergasted brain. Everything came out now in a rush. "One of the wounded men who came home said that . . . he said at Fredericksburg, on that hill, my brother screamed out that everyone was going to get killed and that the rest of our army had already run away. They said you called him a liar and a traitor and ordered him to be arrested!"

"Well, someone did stand up and shout that. But I'm certain it wasn't Peasley. I would have known his voice. And as for ordering that other man's arrest, whomever he was, I wouldn't have gone through with it. I just wanted to confuse any enemy who might be listening in. Can't you give me the name of the soldier who told you this?"

"Corporal . . . ? I . . . I just know the first name— Silas."

"Oh, that one. Well, if I remember correctly, there was bad blood between them over a young lady, I understand. A schoolteacher, wasn't it?"

"Yes!"

A tremendous roar of many cannons drowned Caleb out. The colonel rushed from the tent shouting, "Men into formation!" Hurrying after him, Caleb saw a general gallop up, looking angry and frustrated and snorting like his horse.

"Colonel, I am so tired of blunders that I cannot tell you! Do you see that hill standing all by itself down there at the far end of our defense line? That one big ugly hcap, Little Big Top, is the key to this battlefield. If the enemy captures that and hoists their cannon on top of it, they'll blow to pieces all our defenses on the ridge and roll up our whole army like a rug! Then the battle's lost—and so, most likely, is the war! You take your regiment up the top and cover the south face of it. I'll swing the rest of the brigade around to the west."

The general and his flagman galloped off to the front of the four regiments under his command. The colonel was already rushing forward to lead his men. To Caleb, there seemed to be no need for one more drum. He dropped it as he ran. The rifle was enough.

Bombs were already smashing into the trees when Caleb began to climb. There was a rush of wind against his face. He felt the ground jolt, and from somewhere above him a branch twisted off. Sliding, crashing sounds made him duck below the ledge of a big boulder—but an officer seemed to be yelling at him:

"No time for taking cover, men! Count yourselves lucky we're being bombed. Gives us a chance to get into position up there before the rebs come at us!"

The cannon fire was coming from the top of another ridge that the enemy had captured the day before. Scurrying now among the rocks, Caleb caught glimpses in the distance of white flashes.

What he could not see through all the trees and the thick red smoke were the many thousands of enemy infantry who had already come down from those heights to storm other parts of the Union line. For him, the whole world had shrunk to this one hill where his life might end while he was still going on fourteen.

But Caleb right now was more excited than afraid. This time at least he hadn't been caught by surprise. He had a chance to fight back. And this was where a Peasley belonged. Here, with the Twentieth Maine!

There were ten companies in the regiment, each with a sergeant in charge. One of them tapped him on the shoulder, and Caleb joined his men as they spread out to crouch among the rocks. Other than a pounding in his heart loud enough to hear, there was no sound. The cannon had fallen silent.

"They'll be coming now, men!" called the colonel from somewhere above and behind him. "Tell yourselves there can be no retreat. No surrender. Whatever may happen to us, we must hold this hill!"

Yet the moments stretched out and nothing, not even a squirrel moved down below in the small rocky valley between this hill and a larger one. "Maybe they aren't coming at all," he muttered hopefully. What time was it getting to be? He couldn't tell exactly because the sun was on the other side of Little Round Top. Probably about four. Back home his mother would be getting up the soup for supper. Grandpa would be dragging his rocking chair under him into the kitchen for supper. If things had gone well with the fishing, his father would be heading back into the bay.

It was happening! From behind that other hill, the enemy regiments came on the run—and with bayonets gleaming they shrieked their wild fighting cry. Caleb had been spared hearing that terrifying sound back at the time of the ambush when he'd been underwater. But now, as these never defeated warriors crashed into the underbrush, his body turned electric. The current went up his back, lifting the hair on his neck. His mouth went dry. He couldn't swallow; but along with the other defenders, he fired down at the madly climbing men.

Bullets whistled past him to shatter, ping, and crash against rock. There was a different kind of sound when flesh and bone was struck. He heard the startled gasp of a man nearby being hit and the loud moan that another one made. Those noises gave way, as pressure built in his brain, to a ringing in his ears so loud that he couldn't tell if anyone in his company was firing back. It gave him the sensation that he was all alone, that there was no one here but himself to fight back!

Most of the swarming enemy soldiers were pausing only long enough to jam in their cartridges, aim, and shoot before climbing on. Others, in an even madder rush, saved their fire and sprang over rocks like mountain goats. Through the growing red smoke of gunfire, Caleb saw a bayonet on a rifle and a hate-twisted face behind it charging straight up at him. He raised his gun to shoot. But it wasn't the fear of dying—it was the idea of killing another human being that froze his finger on the trigger. If he had to do it, he could not look at it! He shut his eyes and fired.

When his lids flew open, the man had sprung the last few feet that brought him up level with Caleb. He'd just missed being hit by the boy's shot and wasn't giving him a chance to reload. But Caleb had no need to reload. With his eyes wide open now, he let go again. A look of amazement spread over the man's face as he fell.

When others came charging behind him, Caleb fired and fired again. Men crumbled before him, and still more came on. To Caleb, the Civil War was only himself and the enemy now. So far, there had been enough breathing spaces to give him just enough time, when he needed it, to duck behind his rock and reload. But when he was given no chance to do it, he stood up screaming—and taking the hot barrel in his hands, swung the wooden butt into the side of a man's head. *Crack!* went the skull, the rebel staggered back, and a bullet from somewhere else carried him down.

The soldier in blue who'd shot the man waved his musket barrel from behind another rock. Caleb no longer felt alone. Hastily reloading, he began firing again.

He had no idea how much time had passed before this first attack was driven back. To his right, a Maine man lay sprawled in death over the rock that had been his position. At his right, a soldier who'd covered him before now sat holding his bleeding side.

"Spread out and fill in the gaps!" cried the sergeant. "Here they come again!"

Caleb sprang to the wounded man's side, just as the rebel yells began again. They may have been as terrible as before . . . and the fear must still have been inside him somewhere . . . but now, somehow, he didn't quite feel it. Though he fought, shot, and brought more men down, it all seemed unreal to him now.

He was troubled by one thought: that he was moving very slowly. Yet actually his body had been working quickly, doing everything it had to do. It was Caleb's mind that was slowing down . . . growing numb to all the horror of "seeing the elephant."

This last charge was beaten back, too. But then there was another and another. Fresh enemy regiments came screaming up the hill after the ones that had been torn to pieces by the Twentieth Maine. But the defenders grew fewer and fewer. Caleb fought like a cornered animal until his special kind of ammunition was gone. When the soldier beside him died, he picked up the man's musket and took his cartridges. These soon gave out, too. Caleb wasn't alone in being short of ammunition. Whenever there was a lull in the fighting, men went scrambling among the bodies to find more.

But even that was getting hard to find.

Behind this part of Little Round Top, meanwhile, the hot July sun was beginning to slant down. The yells of the rebel fighters who'd made this last charge had sounded a little less fierce. Among the enemy dead lying on the slope just below Caleb were a few who had their faces turned up. Now that the rage had gone out of them, they looked to him like people he might have known back home. He began to wonder about their ages and where they came from. He was losing his numbness, and he didn't like that—because what took its place was a deep, deep sorrow.

That frightened him. How was he going to keep on fighting if he felt like this? And yet, when there was practically no more ammo to scrape up, Caleb was almost glad of it.

"Fix bayonets!" came the command.

With his ear still ringing, he wasn't sure what he heard. Caleb looked around. Everyone was rising from behind the rocks. An officer rushed over. "Next wave that comes up here we're done for, soldier! Fix bayonet. We're charging them!"

When Caleb fumbled, the officer grabbed his weapon. "Not that way! Like this!" Slapping the bayonet into place, he shoved the musket back. Then he caught a look in the young boy's eyes. "But stay here if you can't do this."

Caleb drew himself up straight. "Who says I can't!"

123

"All right then, let's go!"

The Union soldiers had found a terrifying yell of their own. Caleb, running, tripping, and crashing through brush, screamed it with them. Together with the others, he fell upon men who could not have expected this. Some fought, but many panicked. They turned and ran or threw up their hands in surrender.

Caleb stood in the middle of this, not quite able to understand. Was the battle over? Was the whole war over? No, he could hear the cannon booming elsewhere. The officer who'd helped Caleb fix bayonet took him by the arm and led him aside.

"Colonel tells me your name is Peasley."

Caleb set his teeth. "Yes, sir. That's right, sir." *Officer or not,* he told himself, *this man had better not insult my brother.*

"Saw how you fought. Jonathan would be proud of you. I wanted to ask you what happened to him?"

"We don't know."

"Then he was probably captured."

"Captured?"

"Well, I'd rather believe that than think of a dear friend as dead. Listen, I want you to go with the detail that's taking the prisoners in."

"Look, don't worry about me. If there's going to be more fighting I can handle it!"

"Get!"

10

With their hands clasped behind their heads, the captured soldiers walked slowly through the Union camp. There were so many of these ragged men in gray— nearly four hundred of them—that Caleb was afraid at first that they would try to break away from the small number of men in blue herding them along.

But defeat was on their faces as they shuffled along with their eyes cast down. Only one voice broke their silence. The oldest among them was talking to himself, muttering as if in a daze into a beard as white as General Lee's, "I kain't believe I done surrendered. I kain't believe I done surrendered. I kain't be—"

"Uncle Ezra, there just warn't no other choice fer us," a young prisoner finally said to soothe him. "Besides, you hear all that racket and ruckus back on the ridge up to the town? Why, this here battle ain't over yit by a dang sight."

"It is for you!" roared the corporal in charge of the detail. "Cover me!" he ordered a few of the guards. And pushing into the crowd, he slammed the barrel of his musket deep into the young man's stomach. With a grunt of pain, like the sound of wind rushing out of a bag, the prisoner fell to his knees, grasped his stomach, and doubled over.

The corporal stood over him, raging, "Who told you to put your hands down? Get them back behind your head!"

All the rebels stopped moving at the same time. Many pairs of eyes, that till now had been staring only at the ground, glanced sideways. "Easy does it, Yank," someone said slowly. "We'uns ain't making no trouble."

"Sure you are! Just by opening your mouths! I don't like listening to traitors!"

From somewhere in the middle of the prisoners a voice declared, "Got a country of our own, Yank, and we're loyal to that."

"Which of you said that?"

"We're all a-saying it," someone else called out—and the men in gray began to stand taller.

"Well, I guess somebody needs a lesson here," the corporal growled in a voice as dark as death. He turned back to the vomiting young man. "I ordered you to put your hands up. Too bad you wouldn't listen." He brought his rifle up to eye level.

Caleb stepped in front of the gun.

"You're in my way, Private!"

"This is wrong."

The corporal spat on the ground. "I don't know you. Seems to me, I don't remember you being around this regiment before. How long have you been in this war, sonny boy?"

"Not long, but—"

"Then stay out of this! Hear me? You ain't lost all your friends."

"My brother might be a prisoner of war, just like them."

"That so? How do you think they treat our boys when they catch them?"

Caleb had no answer to give. But while he blocked the corporal's way, other prisoners were moving to lift the injured rebel to his feet. They put his hands behind his head and stepped away from him. When next the corporal looked over Caleb's shoulder, the young man was standing there, swaying. There was nothing to do but signal for the march to begin again. But now everyone in Caleb's detachment was sharp-eyed, finger on the trigger and expecting trouble. At the slightest hint of it, the boy knew, they would begin to fire at these unarmed men. If they did, the boy began to ask himself anxiously, would it be his duty to fire, too?

As they all walked along, a man with a face as crinkled by sun and wind as Caleb's father's slid over to him as closely as he dared. "It were a good thing you done, Yank," he said quietly. "Where you fum?"

Caleb wasn't sure he wanted to talk, but the fellow gave him a friendly smile. "Maine."

"Fum all the way up thar?" repeated the man in a louder voice. "Well, you fellers that come out of Maine sure 'nuff took us old boys from Alabama by surprise. Never knowed there was any Yanks could fight like that." He turned to his comrades. "Ain't that right, gentlemen?"

First there was silence. Then came replies of "Guess so."

"Yep."

"Got to give 'em that."

127

The leather-faced man turned back to Caleb with an easy smile. ''Thar you go.''

The other guards relaxed their trigger fingers just a little bit. Caleb saw a few of the prisoners take deeper breaths. ''How you doing?'' he asked the youth who was walking along, still half bent over.

The rebel youth glared at him. ''How does it look, Yank?''

An icy feeling shot through Caleb's own stomach. So there had been some buttering up, but that's all that it was. The enemy was still the enemy—and maybe the corporal was right to hate them as he did.

He looked up ahead. There were clusters of tents and the supply wagons and the circles of artillery that had not yet gone into the battle, but lay so close to it. Farther on, there was a big rambling fence, and behind it, on a green hill, a lot of cows who weren't paying any attention to the sound of bombs and gunfire a mile or so away.

''Bring 'em to that empty barn,'' said the only officer waiting beside the open gate. ''Search each one before sending him inside. Then stand guard outside till relieved.''

''What are you talking about!'' demanded the corporal. ''We've got to get back to our regiment. Where are all your provosts who are supposed to handle this?''

''Out scouting for more places to keep prisoners. These are yours.''

Caleb was among the soldiers who made them turn out their pockets and patted the inside of their clothes for hidden knives, pistols, even matches.

''Y'all done a right thing fer me back there,'' said the young man. ''But I never talked to no Yankee afore—an' I was feeling real bad. I want to thank you.''

128

"That's all right."

"Your brother a prisoner?"

"Maybe. I'm not sure. Better move on. We're holding up the line."

"Like a chaw of my tobacker? It's real fine. Sure bet they don't grow none like this up here."

Caleb was about to shake his head, but a broken off piece was already being offered to him. He took it before turning to the next man.

It was growing dark, and the sweat that had dried on his clothes left him feeling cold. The men jammed into that barn would at least be warm, he thought, but Caleb had no blanket.

"Cabot! You and Heap go take down some of those fence posts to build a fire."

"But we ain't on rebel land anymore, Corporal. It's a Union farm."

"All the more reason to give to the war effort. Now boys, there's a Union cow or a hog round here with Twentieth Maine written on it. Three of you get that, too. Move. The rest keep an eye on this barn door. It won't be none too strong if they rush it. Tonight nobody sleeps."

His roving eye picked out Caleb, and he walked over. "You keep looking at that plug of tobacco in your hand like you ain't going to use it."

"No."

"Mind if I have it?"

Caleb wondered if he should mention who gave it to him. Instead, he just held it out.

The corporal popped it into his mouth, but then he didn't go away. "I'm glad you stopped me back there."

Caleb nodded. "I'm glad you're telling me."

It was an hour or so before a pig was brought back,

and another two or three before the men began to eat it. "Wonder if they can smell this in that barn," someone said.

"If they can, it'll be driving them crazy."

"Fine with me. A lot of good men died today."

There was a loud rapping on the door. A voice that Caleb recognized as belonging to the leather-faced man called out for the corporal. Everyone watched him walk over slowly. "What do you want?"

"How about some food?"

"In the morning, maybe, when the provosts get back."

"We got some sick and hurt in here. That boy's been throwing up bad."

"Don't know where to find any doctors. Is that about it?"

"No! Leastways let us come out one by one to do our business so we don't make no mess in here."

"Sorry. That's another service we don't provide in this here hotel."

"Then take that boy you done plowed in the stomach out of here for a spell!" cried the man inside angrily. "He's throwing up something fierce. Blood, too."

"I'll watch him!" exclaimed Caleb, springing to his feet before the corporal could refuse.

The corporal wagged a finger at him. "All right, but if he gets away from you, I'm gonna see you go to trial— and then you are one dead soldier! You understand me?"

Caleb nodded.

The guards took positions in front of the big door, ready to fire. Those inside were ordered to stand back, and it was opened a crack.

The young soldier from Alabama came out still in a half crouch. His face was sweating, but in this cool night

130

air he would soon be chilled. Caleb thought of leading him to the fire, but he worried about keeping him near the corporal. Besides there were questions. . . .

"This way," he said, pointing at the gently sloping pasture with his gun. "Keep ahead of me, and move slow. You give me trouble, I'll have to shoot."

"I know that."

They were in open ground now, away from the barn and a farmhouse that showed no lights. "How was the chaw?" the rebel youth asked over his shoulder as they took slow steps under the starlight.

"Didn't try it yet."

"Fust time's the hardest. Gives a shooting feeling into the sides of your jaw, like something you et was real sour."

"Oh, I've done it before. I just don't like it." He didn't mention that his mother thought it was a disgusting habit and had banned it from the house.

"Uh-huh. How old are you anyways, Yank?"

"Old enough, Reb."

"Heck, I know that part fer sure."

"I'm going on fourteen. You?"

"Sixteen," the rebel hissed from between suddenly gritted teeth. "Got to sit down."

They had come to a stand of trees. When the prisoner slid down along a trunk, the shadows blotted out the stars so that they could not be seen from the fire. Caleb didn't like this. But the young man sat rocking back and forth, holding his stomach, making groaning and vomiting sounds.

"I can see it hurts real bad," he said.

"Comes and goes," gasped the boy. In spite of the cool air, he wiped a sweating face. "When it comes,

131

feels like my gut done exploded. Reckon something's broke. Sure glad, though, they's no doctor here. I seen how they took care of the fellers down to Fredericksburg. They'll kill a man afore his time.''

"Did you see any Union prisoners when you were there?"

"Sure did, down to the town, lots of 'em. Maybe not so many as here, though. . . ." His voice trailed away. "I don't hear hardly no fighting going on. You reckon it's all over?"

"I don't know. Where did they send those men? Do you know?"

"Well, they's a prison house in Richmond. But we caught us so many Yanks afore that it was all filled up, what I heard say. They's another one I know of down to a place in North Carolina. That's most likely it."

"How would I—? How would somebody get to it?"

The boy gave him a long look in the darkness. "You want me to take you thar?" He stood up.

" 'Course not!" flashed Caleb. "Sit down, and don't do that again."

"Kain't blame a feller, can ye?"

"Guess not."

"I don't mean no disrespect here, but it could be you know a lot less 'bout your Yankee prisons than I do. They was some part of all right at first, when we used to trade off prisoners. But now nobody comes out of thar. They's too ashamed to show what a man looks like when he's been in awhile. You kin see the bones stand out on him, 'cause they starve him so. That's if he gotten through all the whippin's and the sickness and all—which ain't too likely."

"Either somebody's been lying to you or you're just

making this up! Maybe that what's you people do to your slaves, but we don't do it to anybody!"

"Maybe you wouldn't," groaned the rebel. "But they's others like that corporal." He looked away. "Let's talk some on somethin' else. When it comes to slaves, I never done treated any good or bad. My family never did have any. We always done every last thing fer ourselves on that farm. We was always too poor to do it any other way."

"So then how do you feel about slavery?"

"I reckon I don't think or care about it one way or t'other."

"So why are you fighting?"

"Why? Why did you Yankees come down after us?"

"To save the Union!"

"That's the reason why y'all kilt off my three brothers?"

"Three?"

"That's right. There ain't none left but me."

"That man you called Uncle Ezra . . .?"

"His sons is gone, too. Why do you think his mind done cracked in his brain after he seed he surrendered just to save his own life? He ain't never going to be able to live with that. He ain't never going home, but I am!"

"Hey! What are you doing?"

"Just what you see. I'm a-standing up, and I'm going." Holding his sides, he started to walk.

"No, you're not! You sit down! I told you to sit down."

"You want t'kill me, Yank, then go ahead and do it."

Caleb snapped up the rifle. "I will if I have to. Don't make me have to!"

"Well, y'all do what you have t'do, an' I'll do the

133

same. Iffen you want to shoot a man in the back when he's a-goin' home, you won't never get a better chance at it.''

The rebel was taking long strides for the fence. Caleb hurried after him. ''You said 'going home'—was that what you said?''

The rebel whirled around and stopped. ''I already done my fightin'. Look at me! You don't see that? But you can kill me now and be done with it 'cause I ain't a-going to no prison camp!''

Caleb heard shouts. Some guards were running toward them, taking aim. The rebel, too, saw them coming. Backing away, he turned and made a hobbling run for the fence.

''Fall down!'' whispered Caleb heavily, then fired right past him. But the fleeing soldier either hadn't heard or wouldn't listen. He was nearly at the fence.

Caleb dashed after him, ramming down another cartridge. The rebel was reaching the fence. Caleb looked over his shoulder; the other guards were taking aim.

''Fall down!'' Caleb repeated as loudly as he dared—and shot again.

The rebel's arms flew out to the side as his body arched, and he toppled to the ground.

Before anyone else could draw near, Caleb sprang to the body. ''Promise me to God you won't fight any-more!'' he murmured, while nudging it with his foot and acting as if he was aiming a ''finishing shot.''

Through lips that didn't move came a whispered, ''I promise.''

Caleb took a step back and fired into the ground. Then he walked quickly toward the soldiers coming up.

"Didn't want to, but I had to!" he shakily cried. "It's not the same as fighting."

"Sure it is," declared the corporal, casting a look beyond him at the body.

Caleb walked back with them to the fire.

There they crouched until daylight, when a group of provost guards came to round up the prisoners and take them elsewhere. Caleb was afraid as he left with the detachment that somebody would take a glance, in passing, at the spot where he'd pretended to kill the rebel. When none of them did, he breathed easier. He had gone back in the middle of the night to give the man his blue army cap to wear as a partial disguise while sneaking off. But the fellow was already gone.

They didn't find their regiment back on Little Round Top. Nor was it up on top of that long ridge where thousands of men in blue waited behind piled up rocks for the next attack. The badly shot up Twentieth Maine, they finally learned, were being kept "in reserve" on the slope just below the center of the ridge. The troops, with their rifles stacked nearby, were squatting on the ground, doing their best to relax and hoping not to be needed.

"Well, they certainly did us a favor, putting us here," Caleb heard a lieutenant telling a sergeant sitting on the ground between them. "The center of our lines is the last place in the world where Lee is ever going to attack."

The lieutenant was wrong, but he didn't live long enough to think about it. The first shells that Lee's cannons sent whining through the air were aimed too high for the defenses on the ridge. Down they fell upon the resting men of the Twentieth Maine. And it was the first one to blow up that, as soldiers say, had that officer's "name written on it."

It would have killed Caleb, too, if that sergeant, a man he'd never seen before, hadn't quickly thrown himself spread-eagled over the boy.

The weight of a two-hundred-pound man flattened him like a bug against the shuddering ground. His human shield muffled the roaring, but he could feel the thuds one after another, and some coming together. The pounding went on and on. The man above him lay unmoving and seemed to grow heavier. Caleb felt something wet and sticky dribbling down his face, into his mouth. It tasted salty. Blood.

Was it his own or . . .?

Even if the bombs were still raining down, the thought of lying beneath a dead man was too much. He tried to push himself up, but it was like lying under a boulder.

Thud. Thud. More thuds. But now they grew distant. Rebel cannons were finding their true targets. How long he'd lain there, meanwhile, and how he managed to breathe, he didn't know. Others had to lift the sergeant off him. When they did, and Caleb saw, he broke into tears.

"Not your fault," someone told him. "He probably wouldn't have been able to save himself anyway."

Maybe so, he thought. But what had that to do with it? This man he didn't know had protected him like a father. *I have to bury him myself!*

Another soldier helped him carry the body to a wheelbarrow at the bottom. No officer called out to stop him from going off with it toward the rear. From a supply wagon he took a spade. Finding soft enough earth for a shallow grave, he thought as he dug, of the rebel boy he had saved. Was he himself being spared because he had spared that other boy? But if so, was it fair that God should let him live but not this sergeant? Where was God in all of this, anyway?

He had no answer, and meanwhile, the battle raged on. There was another day of desperate fighting, although Caleb's unit was not in the center of it. It was on the Fourth of July when the exhausted Confederate soldiers who had not been killed or captured walked and limped and carried their wounded away from the battlefield.

Caleb told of the battle in a long letter he wrote to his family. Near the end of it he wrote,

> They say this was a great victory because we beat off all of General Lee's attacks, and he had to go back south. But I *hate* the killing, and the war is still going on! Now we have to chase after the rest of his army, which only means there'll be more fighting. Colonel Chamberlain told me I fought real bravely. Still he said that because I'm so much under age he wanted to get me a discharge to send me home.
>
> But then I told him that as soon as I get it, I'm going to go down to North Carolina to look for Jonathan. He got real upset because he thought it would be a very bad thing to try. I'd made him wonder if he ought not to let me leave the army and only just keep a watch on me whenever he could. I didn't say anything after that, but one way or another, I will do it. You can bet I will! I just have to figure a way that they won't make a mistake like some of them did about Jonathan and think I'm a deserter.

Caleb ended with many apologies for causing so much worry, saying how much he missed them all. He missed the ocean, too! Finishing by the light of a dying campfire, he wrote a short letter to Jonathan's girlfriend, begging her not to listen to that jealous soldier who was trying to steal her away. Then he started one to Melody.

While he was writing those letters he had been seeing those people in his imagination. He didn't notice his loneliness. But he couldn't fall asleep that night, or for many nights afterward, without holding his seashell tightly.

11

Rain soaked the soldiers day after day during the long slow chase after the retreating rebels. Caleb felt as if he were passing under a waterfall and through a swamp. There were times when the mud was so deep and sucked so hard that he would pull out from it barefoot.

His clothes were never dry. He went to sleep under a dog tent wet, woke up wet, and gobbled down wet biscuits as he marched. And he almost never stopped scratching at all the lice that seemed to have taken a special liking to him.

They were slogging along when someone called out, "So, Drummer, what do you think about them little critters making a home on you?"

"Well, they keep me company!" he called back, which brought a big laugh. Caleb was very pleased with this; up in Maine he'd never been much for making jokes.

He was also glad enough that there was so little fighting. The enemy had fewer cannon and supplies to drag along and was moving south much more swiftly. At last, the long march came to a halt near the bank of a river, and the regiments spread out and set up camp. The Twentieth Maine was stationed at a place in Virginia called Beverly Ford. From listening to the men, Caleb now learned that not far down on the other side of the river was the hillside where the battle had been fought in which Jonathan Peasley disappeared.

He went again to see Colonel Chamberlain. "Sir, I request permission," he said, entering the command tent, "to go across and scout the position of the enemy."

The colonel gave him a long look-over. "Worthy try. Permission denied. Dismissed."

But Caleb didn't move.

The colonel leaned back on his canvas chair. "If your brother is dead, they'd have buried his remains by now. The battle was near a town. They wouldn't just leave bodies lying around, even those of the enemy. Besides, what could you recognize after all this time?"

"He used to wear a locket," Caleb said hoarsely.

"And if you don't find it?"

"Then I'm going to go down to that prison camp in North Carolina and find a way to get in and look for him."

The colonel jumped to feet. "That's both insane and impossible!"

"Not if someone can give me a map."

"I couldn't. And I wouldn't. What I *will* do is get you a discharge and send you home. Under guard as far as Washington, if necessary. You will stay in camp until it arrives. If you leave, I'll have you listed as a deserter. From what I've learned of you, son, you certainly wouldn't want to be considered that. Now, I know that men from our state are long on fighting and short on discipline, but this time turn around and march out when I say dismissed!" Gently he repeated, "Dismissed."

Caleb walked away brooding. When he got back to camp, a baseball game was just getting started between his regiment's drummers and the drummers from an Ohio outfit. The other side was loudly complaining because the Maine team, which was short one player, wanted to use one of the regular soldiers. As soon as Caleb came along, a shout went up for him to come out on the field.

"No, thanks," he called back glumly as he kept walking. Two grinning soldiers stepped in front of him. "If you don't play, Peasley, there won't be a show. Now why do you want to go and be the one stone in a basket of strawberries?"

This made it hard to say no. "But I never played it much," protested Caleb weakly. He had spent almost all his long dry summer days catching fish.

"Time you learned, boy! Time you learned!" cried a sergeant, moving in to take him by the shoulders and spin him around. "But learn fast, though! H Company has got its whole month's pay riding on the Fightin' Drummers of the Immortal Twentieth!"

The Immortal Twentieth never finished the game. In the third inning it broke down into a wrestling free-for-all when a Maine boy sprinting toward third base was tripped on purpose by an Ohio infielder.

The cheering soldiers didn't care. They simply changed their bets to who would win the fight. Caleb had stood aside from all this. This fighting was stupid! ALL FIGHTING WAS STUPID! He'd seen enough fighting to last the rest of his life—even if he lived long enough to HAVE A LIFE! This fighting was making him so hopping mad that in another minute he'd show them all just how stupid it really was!

Then all at once, he was wading into the thick of the

fight with a strength he'd never found before, yanking boys off each other and flinging them left and right.

It was at this point that the wildly excited men of the Twentieth declared *him* the winner—and started calling Caleb "Billy Shiloh." This was the nickname of a famous fighting drummer boy in the Union's other army that was doing battle in the west. Now it had spread to become a name given to any drummer that soldiers had decided to treat as a "hero," whether jokingly or for real. Either way, Caleb took no joy in hearing, "Three cheers for our own Billy Shiloh. Hip! Hip! Hurray!"

"I don't want that!" he exclaimed in complete frustration. "I don't need a *third* name. They signed me up into the Fifth Washington by a name I made up! And the Twentieth Maine regiment has me listed by my own! And its weeks and weeks later, but I still haven't gotten a dollar in pay under either one!"

The next morning Caleb awoke to find thirteen dollars in small coins lying on top of his drum. A note came with them saying, "Don't you worry, Caleb Peasley. *We* know who you are!"

Immediately he flew down to the wagons run by storekeepers, called sutlers, who followed the regiments into all their camps. He bought new clothes and a lot of writing paper and ink. There were just enough pennies left over for a few jawbreakers, an apple, a lemonade . . . a used copy of Robinson Crusoe.

For a few days Caleb was almost happy. He filled these days reading his book and writing letters to Melody. Still, he could not shake off a thought growing within him that he was failing Jonathan . . . failing himself.

He stopped enjoying the letters and the novel. This feeling of being sorry for himself was more than a body

142

could stand! He found little things to do. One of them was to go off in search of an old black washerwoman named Beth. She'd been boiling the lice out of soldiers' uniforms and had never returned with his.

The growing city of tents into which the runaway Virginian slaves were jammed lay behind the camps of the nearby regiments. As he walked into it two little children who saw him stopped playing to run screaming for their mamas. People who sat together on empty ammunition boxes talking grew quiet too. When he asked about the washerwoman, they turned away. But a young man, with anger flaring in his eyes, came dashing out of his tent.

"My aunt? She daid!" He planted his hands on his hips and seemed to be waiting for Caleb to start something.

Caleb was confused. Why was he being stared at like that. "Oh, I'm sorry," he said. "How did it happen? Was she sick?"

The young man tossed his head back, snorting, "Not till dem soldiers got through wit her! Den she was sick all right, sick o'livin'—and she give up the spirit an' she died! She was a grandmother and a great-grandmother. She come on her own feets all the way up fum Georgia. Come up here to the *Freedom*, like Father Abraham promised! An' just 'cause she tol' them to be ashamed of themselves for calling her all kind of names an' laughing at her all the time, was that a reason for knockin' her down and stomping her like they done? So you tell me somethin'. How is dem Union boys one thing different from the bosses on the plantation? You tell me dat? I wants to know! I been wonderin' and a-wonderin' why it is I kain't get no answer each time I asks your army to let *me* put on one of dem uniforms so I kin help fight to free my peoples. But I done figured it out why. Dey don't know whut to do wit us, and dey really don't want us free!''

"I do," said Caleb in a low voice. "I know a lot of folks who do."

The angry young freedman wasn't letting him get by with this. "Oh dis is so nice to know. But that bein' so true, then where *is* dey? You think dis was the only time a bad thing was done to somebody here? I disremember how many bad things was done, you count all the whuppings and all the mean and low down things was said. An' all this being cheated out of the few pennies we suppose to get for the work we do for 'em.''

While this was going on, others nearby were frantically waving at the young man to stop. Fear showed in their faces that Caleb would go back to his own camp with stories that would raise more anger against them.

"Don't listen on him," said an old man. "He don't have the sense of a jackass say things like that to a nice gemmen like yourself.''

Caleb had been trying hard to think of what to say. And when he finally did speak, it was to stammer words that sounded stupid even as he uttered them. "I . . . I have a friend who once followed the Drinking Gourd.''

They looked at one another, then at him. "You know what dat means?'' a woman quietly asked.

"Yes, I do, ma'am," Caleb said, tipping his cap.

They were waiting for him to say more. And not knowing what else to do, he told them about Steven Duval. How the self-educated former slave had smuggled Caleb aboard the *Dolphin* in a sack and protected him. He described the secret talks between Wo Fong and Duval about living among white men in the midst of so much unfairness. And he spoke about his own fight with Ship-rat, after the man stabbed Duval, blaming blacks for the war.

"I guess there are Shiprats here, too," he ended by declaring. "But my colonel is a very fair man and a good man. And I am going to ask him about what happened to your aunt and about getting you into the army."

He was approaching the command tent when the colonel saw him coming. Before he opened his mouth, the colonel lifted a hand.

"Don't say a word to me, Private. I can tell everything from that expression on your face that this matter has been eating on you, but I do not want an argument. I have received a letter from your mother. She begs me to convince you that she loves you every bit as much as her other son. I don't know why she thinks that is the role of a colonel in the United States Army to clear up the issue of who is her favorite, but—"

"Why hasn't *she* written to me?" he asked, thoughts of anything else flying out of his head.

"She has. But a letter to me will come quicker, I'm afraid, than one to you. More than anything, she wants you to come home. Does this change your mind about going after your brother?"

Caleb took a deep breath. "No."

"So I expected."

"This has nothing to do with how anybody feels about me," Caleb said almost tearfully. "This is for *him*."

"You realize that you will almost certainly be throwing your life away?"

"I can't let myself think like that."

"No, I suppose not," sighed the colonel. "The discharge papers have arrived and just need my signature.

145

Take them with you when you go over. If you're caught out of uniform, I don't see how they will keep you from being shot as a spy, but . . ." His voice trailed off, and he began again. "Wait until the first rainy night. I'll have someone show you where you can swim across the fastest."

"Thank you, sir!"

Colonel Chamberlain seemed far less happy about this than Caleb. "We will set up a little diversion about a mile farther down." He paused and held out his hand. "You'll have my prayers, Caleb Peasley. That's the best I can do."

When Caleb returned to his tent, he wrote letters to his parents and to Melody. These were words of good-bye, to be mailed by one of his friends among the drummers only if he never came back. It wasn't until he lay down that he recalled his unkept promise to speak to the colonel about the washerwoman's murder. Springing to his feet, he hurried to the command tent, but the colonel was gone.

Freedmen gathered around him when he came back to apologize. They listened in silence to his apology, but when he spoke of going after his brother, help began to pour in.

"Uh-uh, Caleb! Don't go near to that ol' town," one man who'd slaved his whole life near Fredericksburg warned him. "The colonel was right to say you won't find no bodies there. They had us to digging, an' I knows. All their own got buried decent. The Union boys, why, they thrown them under the ground, too, with maybe nothing said over them."

"Now I'm gonna tell you something 'bout what that white skin of yours *won't* do for you," a woman put in.

"Peoples down there don't take kindly to strangers—not any kind. They going ast you all kinds o'questions which you kain't answer. First words leave your mouth, they going to know you don't talk like them. Ain't much time left t'teach you neither, 'cause it goin' rain soon 'nuff!"

"Why kain't he make out to be like ol' Gobo?" suggested the young man who had shouted at him earlier.

"Gobo can't speak."

"What I'm saying!"

The woman grew thoughtful. "Hmm."

"Adam done hit on it!" said the older man.

"Make out he kain't write neither," the young man named Adam went on. "They'll say he ignorant like a *slave* who don't know nothing and ain't worth asking nothing."

"Leave him be, Adam," someone murmured.

But Adam looked Caleb over slowly. "If you going to get away wit dis, you kain't strut your stuff in good clothes and new shoes just bought from a wagon. Specially no *northern* shoes, or they ketch you right there. Whut you need is some plantation massa's old throwaways an' coveralls wit holes in dem, jest like mine."

Several people shot hard looks at the young man. "Don't you go giving him yo' nice things," one of them warned Caleb.

"But I'll bet he's right. Adam, where can we go to trade."

Adam pointed at a tent. " 'Step in there,' said the spider to the fly." He flashed a smile as he followed Caleb inside. "They say the Yankee traders are the best. How'm I doing so far?"

Caleb grinned back. "I wouldn't want you to be any better."

After the trade came lots of Do's and Don'ts from all sides about safely getting all the way down through Virginia to North Carolina—a week's walking in the nighttime.

"Don't start headin' straight south. Go out to where the mountains start, and then keep the mountains to the side of this shoulder." Caleb's right arm was tapped. "Be harder to walk in them foot hills—but that is wilder country and got less people to mind you' business."

"Throw a rock into a cave t'see if a bear be home. You don't get no answer, you still can find two sweet little cubs all alone in there. If you do, git out fast 'cause mama's always coming home."

"Don't go lying down in no hay barns in the daytimes, even if you don't hear dogs barking. Same thing's true for any cotton-gin houses, only double."

"The high grass is good for gettin' out of the way of the daylight by layin' down. But watch out fo' steppin' on snakes."

"If you hear any kind of dogs, get to water fast so they don't follow you."

"If they is a cornfield that ain't been picked over yet, it could mean the white menfolks is all gone to the war. Don't take no chances, though, making fire. Corn that ain't cooked is the best eating anyways."

"Anything a deer will come up to steal out of a garden, nobody will go lookin' to ketch them some man. But when you take a melon, big thing like that, never leave no parts of it laying 'round. Some hound dog named Blue is goin' to sniff 'round, get a smell on you—an' that is trouble."

"If you starving bad 'nuff to take a chance, why, being white like you is, go up nice and easy to the farmhouse

148

kitchen door. Show the lady you ready to fetch water, chop her wood. If she starts some long praying over you at supper an' givin' you a big sermon 'bout not leadin' a sinful life no more, act real sorrowful. You might get youself a dollar, too—maybe.''

A finger wagged under his noise. "But if you come to a black folks' cabin, don't you go playing no dummy games on them. They done seen one trick or 'nother all their lives, and they spot you right out fo' a liar. Talk up an' tell the whole truth. Except if the lady's hoecakes don't taste real good. Most ladies set big store by how their hoecakes are 'preciated.''

Caleb certainly was glad for all the advice. But alone in his tent back in the soldiers' camp, he couldn't lie to himself. The more he thought about his chances, the more frightened he grew. He was thankful for each night that it didn't rain, but only sprinkled a drop or two before stopping. And meanwhile, he worked on a letter to the colonel.

He'd started it by explaining about the young freedman who wanted to fight for his people and have justice for his aunt. But with so much time on his hands the letter grew into a plea for understanding of all those men, women, and children he'd met in that tent city who had stopped being slaves . . . but had yet to be free. At last the evening came when it poured. He delivered the letter to the colonel, and they shook hands, then he walked out to the tent city to make his good-byes.

Adam went down to the water's edge with him, but not to the narrow part of the river the captain had pointed out. This was exactly where three runaway slaves had been shot while trying to get to the Union lines. Most likely there were slave catchers hiding by the other shore

149

right now—even if they were looking for people coming in the opposite direction.

Although the colonel had already started his "diversion" downstream, shooting up flares and having some muskets fired, they crept upstream to a deeper and faster part of the river. Adam tied the end of a very long piece of rope around a tree. Next he fastened the end of a second long rope around another tree about eight feet away. He had Caleb stand between the trees, facing the river. Then he pulled one rope down to Caleb on the left and the other down to Caleb on the right.

"Never ast you if you kin swim," he said.

"I can."

"Don't matter anyhow. Somebody see you pushing water around, you dead in one shot. You got to walk across on the bottom. Problem is, though, it so easy down there get turned round and go the wrong way without you knowing it. Some turtle snap at you an' you jumps. Or you stumbles on some big rock an' you twists . . . Anything like dat. So you keep both these ropes tight in front of you. You lets them play out through yo' hands and between your feets as you goes along. If one of them ain't tight in your hand you knows you going wrong way, you starting t'turn back. Understan' what I'm saying?"

Caleb nodded. "And I hold this reed in my other hand to breathe through?"

"You be breathing water through it we don't tie the top of it to this here little stick. You ready now?"

Caleb took a deep breath for more than one reason. "Guess I am."

They shook hands, and he walked into the water, feeling it coldly rise up around him . . . then close over his head.

12

Almost from the start things went differently from the way he'd planned. A powerful underwater current twisted the trailing part of one of the ropes around his leg. As he tripped on it the reed through which he'd been sucking air bobbed under and some water he wasn't ready for poured through it. Between coughing the water up and spinning around to free himself, he lost direction. Now there was no choice but to swim up to the surface.

Under a rain-swept sky, he located the dark shore and dived underwater again. Rising and ducking a few more times until his hands touched ground, he came out on all fours scrambling fast for the trees. Suddenly a long rifle barrel pushed out of a clump of bushes and up against his nose. Standing over him was a man in a wide-brim hat and rain slicker. Another man appeared behind him holding a length of chain.

"Aw tarnation, he's white!" the first man cried in frustration. "He's white as you'n me! There ain't no reward money fer this one!"

"See maybe if he's got some in his pocket," said the other.

"Shucks, look at him! He's dressed worse as some nigra boy."

"That don't make no never mind. Here now, you, empty them pockets! But move your hands slow like." All that fell out of Caleb's torn coveralls was the seashell and his soaked discharge paper. The man with the chain picked it up and opened it. "Whut is this here now, Zeke?"

"How'm I suppose to know when I kain't read a lick no more'n you. Looks some official though."

"This here boy is some pore," the man with the gun grumbled. "Whatever did we want to watch anybody coming *this* way for?"

"Because he might could be a spy."

"A *spy?* Why shore! You could be right! Here now, boy, you a spy?"

Making a gurgling noise, Caleb pointed to his throat.

"Speak up, sonny. Or I'll blow you apart right here."

"I'm not a spy."

"That right? Well then, they ain't no money in you a'tall. Say your quickest prayer, 'cause you a goner." He cocked the gun.

"I *am* a spy!"

"Hear that brother? We in business! Tie him up real good, and let's be on our way."

Bound hand and foot, Caleb was thrown like a sack of meal into a wagon and driven away. Perhaps it was half an hour later, when he heard, "Halt! Who goes there?"

"Two good old boys who caught us a Yankee spy swimmin' over the river 'bout two miles above Beverly Ford. We goin' see your captain."

"Maybe later, but right now seeing this corporal is the

best you kin do," said another voice that made Caleb instantly lift his head. "What's that you're a-holding?"

"This here is what we found on him. Some kind of shell is what it looks like. Though we s'pect it's something to do with a . . . a secret code, don't you know. And this here official kind of writing, that's a federal eagle on it, ain't it?"

There was a long pause, then Caleb heard that same familiar voice having trouble sounding out the words, "Private Will . . . iam Strong, also known as Cal . . . eb Peas . . . ley, drum . . . mer, who was latc . . . ly at-attached to the Twen . . ."

Caleb called out, "You promised me to God you'd go home to Alabama and wouldn't fight anymore!"

He heard splashing in the rain. Suddenly the rebel prisoner he'd saved was standing over him goggle-eyed. "Whut are you doing here?"

"Got my discharge for being too young. And I'm going down to that place in North Carolina you said to look for my brother."

"Not me, you dern fool! I never told you to *go* there! Now look at the trouble you in. How'm gonna get you out of this?"

"Soldier, you ain't!" cried one of the slave catchers. "This here is a hundert percent damn Yankee spy. An' if you don't want him, we goin' take him some other part o'this army if we has to sell him to General Lee hisself. Giddap!"

The corporal jumped back. "Hold it right there, or we'll blow your fool heads off." Caleb heard the snap of rifles.

"Now, see here, this is business!"

"Yes, and doing our duty to our country, too," put in the second man.

A horse trotted up, it's rider glancing down at the prisoner. "Corporal, what in the world is going on."

"Cap'n, this here is the Union feller who stood in front of a gun to keep me from bein' kilt whilst I was a prisoner. Saved my life a-gettin' away, too."

"He's one of us at heart, then?"

There was a pause. "No, I'm not," Caleb said quietly.

"Cap'n, I think it was because of my three brothers. He was a-worrying about my ma, I guess. His own brother is maybe a prisoner since Fredericksburg."

"I'll look into this."

Taken from the slave catchers, Caleb was kept under guard until the captain returned from a talk with the regimental colonel. Then he was taken to the command tent.

"I suppose you don't know Colonel Chamberlain personally?" he was asked.

"Sir, he's been real kind to me. So, in a way, I do know him a little."

"I understand Chamberlain was never a soldier before. That he used to be a professor?"

"I think so."

"Well, if it weren't for that college professor and the great skill and bravery of you men . . . and boys . . . from the Twentieth Maine, we would have taken that hill and the battle might have gone differently. Now our chances of winning this war don't quite look the same. So, you are looking for your brother. I can understand that. I can no longer look for mine. John was killed by a bullet that perhaps *you* fired." He fell silent for a moment, sighed, and continued. "For your own good, I'm going to send you back across the river."

"Thank you, sir, but I'd rather go on, sir."

"I know." The colonel gave a little smile. "Well, here's your shell. I suppose it reminds you of home? Mine, I haven't seen in two years. Take your discharge paper, too." He smiled a bit wider this time. "Colonel Chamberlain thinks of everything, it seems. This is a nice legal trick to keep you from automatically becoming a spy when you were caught out of uniform. Send him the appreciation of Colonel William C. Oates of the Fifteenth Alabama."

Caleb had never known the name of the rebel private, now a corporal, that he had saved. "It's Henry Wilheight," he was told as they went off together. "An' about my promise? That warn't any real one, on account of I had my fingers crossed all the time."

"Doesn't make it right," said Caleb, glancing at half-burned bushes and trees that had already been blown apart during earlier battles.

"Lucky for you I was here when you needed me, though."

"That's true. But a promise to God is still a promise."

"Couldn't help it. You call me a rebel, but this is my country." He stopped. "Anyways, we're here."

Caleb looked about. "I don't see the river."

"No, but that's a road yonder that hardly nobody uses since the last time there was fighting round here. Below that they's an awful dark woods called The Wilderness. I allow as how it's chock full of spooks an' haints. But they ought to keep you a-movin'. Head south by the sun, and iffen you don't get lost, you'll make it, I reckon it's 'bout twenty miles. After that, you're on your own in open country. Might be you could hop a train below Richmond a-goin' south. Here's a few—mighty few—

Confederate dollars. I think you crazy as all get out to be a-going down to a prison. In case you ain't figured it out yet, some folks who watches prisoners get mighty mean real quick when they see how easy it is to get away with doin' anything they want to somebody else. Well good luck to you, Yank! Lose the war, and go home safe!''

"Same to you, Reb!''

They shook hands and parted.

Caleb found no ghosts in the forest. But the woods were dank, and the ground sent up steam in the blazing summer heat of the day. His already torn coveralls took a few more rips from briars—and meanwhile, his hunger grew. He was still in The Wilderness when he slumped against the trunk of a tree that night and went to sleep.

The first long moan—*Waaaoouuu*—made his eyes pop open. "Probably just an owl,'' he said. Still, there were different wails afterward—and no dreams that could be called good ones. The next morning he tried to beat out the squirrels chasing for nuts. But the few mouthfuls he got did very little to drive away memories of sizzling bacon on blueberry flapjacks soaking in maple butter . . .

Open farming country at last! But wherever he passed, the corn had been picked already . . . and a body couldn't get any nourishment from stuffing his mouth with cotton. He was holding his groaning stomach when he came across four women in clothes the colors of the rainbow who were trying to push a covered wagon out of the mud. Without being asked, he threw himself into it and got rewarded with a big candy apple and a ride heading south.

The ladies soon realized that he could not speak (he'd decided to try that again) and gave up asking questions.

Caleb slept a good deal, getting up only to help build a roadside fire when it was time to cook.

The food was different from any he'd ever had, and for the most part the women talked to each other in a language he could not understand. Grandpa Peasley would have known what it was at once, he thought. Probably understood some of it, too. He guessed from the crystal balls packed away inside—and from some strange-looking playing cards—that they were gypsies. The oldest of them, a heavy woman with black curls and flashing teeth, decided to read his fortune and reached for his hand.

"You will become," she said touching the lines in his open palm, "a great man with a silver tongue and a golden voice. Oh, yes, my handsome, you will speak like a poet! Women will adore you! But for you, only one will make your heart sing. Only one will put her melody in your soul!"

Startled, he tugged his hand away. The woman leaned back in her folding chair. "What? You do not like girls yet?" She searched his eyes more closely. "O-ho! So you know her already!"

Caleb jumped off the wagon.

"Come back, my handsome, and I will make no more fun of you."

Caleb kept on walking, but once he stopped being angry, he realized that he stood more chance of being captured while on his own than disguised as one of them. That night he overtook them by a roadside fire. They invited him to eat, gave him many smiles. And the next morning he drove off with them, wondering if and when he should make a miracle happen—and speak.

Meanwhile, they decided that they didn't like his

157

clothes and gave him others to wear, tight black pants and a white fluffy shirt with all sort of lace on it. He felt much more embarrassed going into a town dressed like this than he would have done in Adam's rags. But they sent him into the barber shop to dole out printed copies of this ad to everyone inside:

GENTLE MEN, WE ARE HERE AT LAST!
THE FOUR KARMOZOFF SISTERS
WE KNOW ALL, SEE ALL, TELL ALL
FROM THE FAR CORNERS OF THE EARTH WE COME
STRAIGHT FROM THE CROWNED HEADS OF EMPIRES
TO YOU
WE OFFER FOUR READINGS AT ONE TIME, COUNT THEM!
WITH TEA LEAVES, CARDS, PALM, AND CRYSTAL BALL
SO CROSS, IF YOU DARE, OUR PALMS WITH SILVER
AND THE FUTURE SHALL BE YOURS!

Then Caleb went into the general store and handed out different fliers to the shopping ladies. This was a town where very little ever happened to excite anyone—and a crowd of curious citizens soon gathered on the street. Watching Caleb's fancy bows and sweeping gestures of welcome, they took their places in line before the beaded curtain at the back of the wagon. He helped the women to step up, then later ran to the front and helped them down when they passed through the wagon to the driver's seat. Many of them found his manners so charming, his smile so "darling," that they crossed his palm, too, saying words like, "Here's a little extra something, dear, just for you." And more than once (this made him want to scream) they told him he was "just as sweet as a sugar plum."

Another week went by while the "Grand Tour" of the Karmozoff sisters through Virginia's little towns continued. The slowness of getting where he was going made him impatient, yet at the same time he was happier sharing the traveling home of these ladies than he'd been in some time.

They were very fun-loving ladies. They could find something hilarious to say about almost anything—though at first it was mostly in their own language. But when they saw him looking left out, they repeated it in English, especially for him. There were times when they were so funny, he had to choke down a roar of laughter that would have instantly given himself away. Other times they cried over his being unable to speak, saying prayers and kissing charms over him. They teased him, too, but it was with love, so that more and more he grew guilty about the lie he was living. And it was just before they entered the first town in North Carolina that he amazed them by beginning to speak—and worried them greatly by telling the entire truth about himself and his dangerous mission. He did it because if he got in trouble, he didn't want the sisters to be part of it.

The ladies pleaded with him, yet he would not change his mind. In the end they took him to within twenty miles of the army prison. They gave him his rags back and some money and more kisses than he could stand, and they drove away wiping their eyes. Caleb moved on.

Just before crossing a railroad track hours later, he passed a row of tumble down shacks. Most had clothes stretched out to dry in the sun. Above the door of one of them was a wooden cross. An old black man, with a minister's collar on his shirt, stood in front of his little church bending over a vegetable garden. Seeing that he was having trouble pulling out a very thick weed, Caleb went over, touched the man's shoulder, then gave the plant a few hard tugs until it came loose.

"Why thank you kindly, suh," said the pastor. "How very nice of you. May I ask where you are from?"

Caleb made a little noise and shook his head.

"You cannot speak?"

Caleb lifted his palms.

"Well then, are you able to write?"

Caleb shook his head.

"No matter. The good Lord gave you a heart that is bigger than all your troubles," said the pastor.

Caleb smiled and walked on across the tracks.

The rest of the little prison town seemed pretty enough, with its shade trees and nicely kept white houses. There was a lovely white church at the other end of Sanderson, and next to that was a cemetery where every grave had a headstone or a cross to mark it. But a mile or so beyond that began another burial ground.

No church was here, nor any stones or crosses—just an open pit about ten feet long and five feet wide. Closer to the road were many mounds of earth covering other pits that had already been filled in.

A few buckboards loaded down with bodies of dead men in Union rags had been drawn up along the side of the road. Caleb saw slaves under guard pulling them off, one by one, and dropping them into wheelbarrows and carting them to the pit. Coming closer, he saw that the faces of those soldiers being dumped inside were hollow. It was if as they had already become skeletons before they died! He could hardly bear to look at them. One of the corpses might be Jonathan!

He felt the need to throw up. He fought it back—and also the growing terror of Sanderson Prison. All these weeks that he had been planning to come here, he'd kept himself from thinking too much about the task in front of him. But now he had to ask himself squarely—how was he ever going to get inside without becoming a prisoner himself? And if he did find Jonathan, how in this world was he going to get him out?

The dark gray prison wall loomed ahead of him. It was about three times the height of a tall man, and nothing could be seen behind it. He noticed rebel soldiers with muskets walking slowly along the top. There were sentry boxes up there, too, where a guard could go to get out of bad weather while he watched the prisoners below. The wall was very long, and nothing could be seen behind it. It went on and on in a straight line until it turned a sharp corner, then another and another until it formed a square that was large enough to cram many thousands of captured men inside. As Caleb drew near to the iron gate he noticed several off duty men leaning against the wall nearby or squatting on the ground smoking and playing cards. They paid him no attention, but one of the two sentries looked him over head to foot and began to chuckle. "I declare, you are some ragamuffin," he said. "What do ye want?"

Caleb made a gurgling little noise, touched his mouth, and shook his head. He had to repeat this several times before the man said: "Whut're you telling me, you can't speak a lick? That it?"

Caleb nodded sadly, then began rubbing his stomach and pretending he was chewing.

"Come a-beggin' fer a handout, have ye?"

Caleb shook his head and made a motion as if he was grabbing a shovel and beginning to dig.

"Oh, ye want a job! At *grave digging?*"

Caleb began to show how fast and hard he would dig, if they let him.

"No, we don't use white folks fer that, not even a dummy like you. So you'd best get on your way, hear? You turn round and go to the church yonder. They won't send nobody away."

But Caleb drew himself up straight and saluted. He saluted again and again until the guard stopped him.

"Wait. You want to jine the army, that it?"

Caleb shook his head and jabbed a finger into his chest and saluted again.

The other sentry caught on. "This feller's telling us he was in the army!"

Caleb nodded happily.

"Well, that's a good'un," the first guard snorted. "They shore must of been scraping the bottom of the barrel wherever that enlistment sergeant gone and took a dummy like this!"

Caleb shook his head and touched his scar. Then he made motions of firing a musket and touched his cheek again.

"You tellin' us now . . ." the second sentry paused to spit out tobacco juice, "that you was all right afore you was shot at?"

Caleb lifted his hands high above his head. He made swooping dives with his fingertips.

"Afore the bombs come down on you?"

Caleb nodded and fell to his knees, clutching his head. The guards had stopped snickering. The off duty men lowered their cards to watch him rocking back and forth.

Moments passed in silence, as if they all had terrible battle memories of their own. Finally one of them said, "What was your outfit, boy?"

Caleb took one of the hands off his head and held up five fingers.

"The fifth? Fifth what? Fifth Tennessee? Fifth Virginia?"

He puzzled over explaining this until the words of a song came to him. Slapping one knee, he pointed at it and began to pluck at an imaginary musical instrument.

"Got it!" bellowed one of the men, delighted at his own brightness. "He was in the Fifth Alabama. You know, 'I come from Alabama with my banjo on my knee'."

Caleb leaped into the air giving a silent Indian war whoop for joy. He came down grinning like a clown at the man who'd figured it out and clapping his hands together.

What might have passed for smiles broke over the stony faces around him. "Well, I don't know as how I believes him," one of the cardplayers declared. "Seems to me they would of sent him on home."

"Lessen he went outen his head and done took off whilst they was fetching him back," another man suggested. "We seen some of *them,* time to time. All a-babbling and not hardly knowing who they is or where they're a-goin'. Here now, what did you do in the army afore you took dumb?"

Caleb made drumming motions.

"That so? Show us, won't ye kindly, on this here water bucket." Spilling it out, he turned the bucket upside down and set it on the ground.

Caleb searched around until he came up with a couple

of sticks. Silently he prayed that the Confederate drum calls were the same as the Union Army's, then he began rapping them out. . . .

"Well, he knows them, for sure," the first sentry declared at last. "An' I guess we oughta do somethin' for him . . ."

He was taken through the gate and then into a low and tiny building just inside of the high wall. The major who was warden of the prison stood over his desk moving papers around. Not once while the guard explained about the boy did this officer look up at either of them.

"Leave him here and go back to your duties," he snapped, and Caleb was left to wait.

Gazing past the man's bent shoulders, he saw through a window a second but lower prison wall. This was a fence of nailed together posts, like the kind of stockade that had been used since colonial days to hold off raiding Indians. The fence posts were as thick as trees, and every one of them came to a point on the top. Those edges looked so sharp that any man trying to escape, thought Caleb, would be speared like a fish on a pike. He guessed that this inside fence must also run all the way around the prisoners, and that it was between the two walls that the guards all lived.

"Can you write?" asked the major, without looking up.

Caleb sadly shook his head.

"Then you're no value to me as a clerk. Well, I have another use for you . . . provided you're willing."

Caleb began to nod his willingness, but the major cut him short. "Wait until I tell you what it is. Your main job is to help the medical officer when he comes here in the morning. Dr. Baines has taken a dislike to living in the quarters here, and he stays in a room at the tavern in town. If he's not here within a few minutes after the bugler blows reveille . . . or if he's still not sober . . . you go out among the prisoners ahead of him to find out who has died during the night. And for each dead Yankee, you will tie . . . Just a moment. . . ." From a large box on the floor he drew a thick handful of red tags with strings. "You will tie one of these on the body. Do you understand?"

Caleb nodded. He understood very well indeed. Here would be his chance to go among the captured men!

"Now this doesn't mean at all that you yourself get to decide who's still living and who is dead. That is for Captain Baines to do. He's goin' to check the pulse and all to make sure nobody is pretending. Your task is only to make sure you locate them all. But you don't have to worry about not being able to talk. Once the Yankees see that you're what they call 'the Deadfinder,' they'll lead you to the new bodies quickly enough. You just attach a tag to the dead man's left wrist, then point him out to the doctor. Later on in the afternoon you find them again for the grave diggers when they come to haul them away. Do you think you can handle it? I have to know now."

Caleb gave another quick nod.

"Well, that's fine, but I don't want to lie to you." He fixed a long look on the boy. "It is the Union's fault, not mine, that these prisoners are not exchanged for our own. Because of that, there is not enough food or medicine to go around. And in their weakened condition they cannot stand up to any illness. There is a lot of sickness beyond the stockade. These diseases become very dangerous very fast, and you could easily catch one. The two men who did this work before are dead. You are sure you're ready to take your chances on that?''

Caleb was as far from being ready as anyone could ever be. Still, he pulled himself together and nodded yet again.

"All right, then. But if I ever find you taking a bribe to make a mistake about whose wrist to tie one of these on, I am going to straighten you out with this revolver by putting a bullet right between your eyes. Is that as clear as can be?''

Caleb nodded that it was.

"Your pay is one half dollar a day, but your food and lodging and suchlike are taken out of that. Any guards who want to give you a few pennies for your special services . . . running errands for them and so on during your free time . . . why, that's up to them, and no questions asked. You are dismissed. Orderly!'' he barked to a soldier just outside the door. "Find an empty bunk for this man in one of the guards' barracks and issue him a uniform, if you can find one.''

As soon as Caleb had settled in, he went to the mess nearest his barrack to join the evening meal. A slave stood behind a table near a campfire serving out beans and black-eyed peas and half-burned horsemeat. Caleb held out a tin plate, wondering what the man was thinking. But when their eyes met for a moment, the slave quickly looked away. Caleb squatted down on a hardwood bench under a shed roof, eating silently while trying to look through the chinks in the stockade fence. He had already begun his search for Jonathan. Yet when he saw a wide open mouth pressed against one of those openings—then another mouth and another—he had to stop chewing and looking.

A cardplayer that he'd seen earlier sat down across from him, blocking his view. "If you've a mind to pass any scraps to them, don't do it," he said, wiping bean gravy onto a slab of corn pone. "Leastways not till ye know who's a-watching. Major Watts, he'd skin ye alive. Well, mebby he wouldn't—seeing you're the new Dead-finder, which is runnin' scarce. The rules is, though, ye can feed the major's hound dogs, but ye *don't* feed his Yankees. He's a man who does a power of hatin', and he wants them to die nice and regular. So ye don't get in the way of that."

Caleb caught himself about to sigh, but the guard had already noticed it, and slowly he said, "I know what you're a-feelin' right now. An' since you're a dummy, I can tell you 'bout me." He leaned partway over the table. "I thought this guard's job would be better than more fightin'. So when my wound healed up, I volunteered for it. But it ain't. Does somethin' to a man, y'know? Do something to you, too. Better hope this war ends soon."

When Caleb nodded, the guard slid his hand across the table, dropping his voice still further. "You're not supposed to take any weapons in there, 'case they get hold of it. But time to time there's men go crazy enough to kill a guard. You take this blade an' keep it up your sleeve."

Caleb hid it away quickly.

13

When the doctor didn't arrive on time in the morning, Caleb went alone through the inner gate. The yard was jammed with prisoners. There were no barracks or sheds in this open field. Nor was there anything that could be called a tent. Sprawled men lay close together on the bare ground. Some of them protected their eyes and faces from the sun by using lean-tos put together out of torn bits of clothes tied to sticks. Others had dug shallow holes for themselves, and as he passed their huddled forms heads popped up like groundhogs.

"Deadfinder!" one of them called in a thin little voice that could have belonged to a very old man or woman. "There's a body stinking bad over here that wasn't taken away yesterday or the day before."

Caleb went over, dreading the thought that this was how he might find his brother. But he could not have recognized anyone from *that* corpse. Not daring to breathe, he bent quickly over it and tied on a tag.

Reaching out of the hole nearby, a hand tugged lightly at the leg of his pants. "You got anything I can eat," the thin-voiced man inside whispered. "Won't tell anybody, I swear!"

Caleb shook his head and walked away. But a few feet further on, he turned back. Kneeling down as if to examine the fellow, he dropped from his pocket the crust of pone he'd been carrying for Jonathan.

When he rose, he caught a glimpse of a guard on the high wall staring at him and shaking his head. Caleb turned away because someone else was calling to him now, pointing to another corpse.

Zigzagging from one to another, Caleb had tagged thirteen bodies by the time he'd come up to a stream of water flowing across the center of the field. Whether it gurgled out of the ground by itself or came through some pipes in the walls, he could not tell. But it smelled like an outhouse toilet, yet there were men crouching down to drink.

On a table nearby stood a few wooden buckets with the day's ration of food. A slave was there to serve out portions, but he had almost nothing to do. Not many of even these starving men could bring themselves to put in their mouths what was inside. Caleb peered into one of the buckets. Hardtack, alive with maggots! The slave must have understood the question in Caleb's eyes, for he said, "The smart ones here, massa, tries to ketch rats instead."

Caleb jumped the stream and moved on. For some reason the prisoners seemed thicker here than on the other side. While looking for more men who were dead he could hardly move without tripping over others who were half alive.

"Deadfinder, you look like someone I knew back home."

That voice gave him an electric shock. *Jonathan! It's Jonathan!*

He looked down on a face so hollowed out at the cheeks that he barely recognized him. But yes, it was his brother, lying on his back, with a tattered blue rag shielding him only slightly from the blinding sun. Caleb stared hard, yet at the same time he did not want to see! He was gazing at skin so thin he could almost look through it to the bones. The once powerful body that had nearly turned to straw. The eyes that used to flash were dull and nearly dead. Finding Jonathan should have been a moment for joy, but such a pang of grief came over him that he knew he must walk on at once—that, or give himself away to those guards on the wall whose glances were always following him.

There was more work to be done. He stumbled through it, tagging bodies—and each of them made him think of Jonathan.

I must get him out! I must. I must!

Meanwhile, he had to give his brother some signal! Some hope. Some reason to keep fighting to stay alive . . .

There were thirty-one bodies in all by the time Caleb was through. Then he turned back, being careful to go the same way. But as he was nearing that tattered bit of blue shirt, he could see that Jonathan was gone!

As disappointed as he felt, he was glad that his brother had been able to get up and move about. It meant that Jonathan still had some strength. Caleb was secretly clutching the seashell he'd removed from his pocket when he'd put away his leftover tags. But were any of the nearest guards closely watching him? Still walking, he drew the back of his arm across his dripping brow.

While wiping the sweat away, Caleb stole a quick look at the high wall—saw one guard talking to another and he pretended to trip. The instant his two hands touched the ground, the palm holding the shell slid it just under the little mound of loose dust and dirt his brother had been using for a pillow.

He moved on, finding another body he had missed along the way. Trembling with a mixture of fear and horror, he went to the stockade's inner gate. As he was being let out, a furious officer grabbed him by the shoulders, screaming, "Next time, you wait for me! Hear? I'm the doctor, not you!"

The corn liquor fumes being blown into Caleb's face made him wince, and at the same time he was being shaken from head to foot. He needed to find some way to steady his mind—and all at once a funny notion came to him. It was of the oldest Karmozoff sister examining the officer's bloodshot eyes as if they were hands and reading his future from the red wavy lines.

"What are you grinning at, you bloody fool! Answer me!"

"Begging your pardon, Captain Baines," offered a guard at the gate. "But this here boy kain't talk."

"Oh." He let Caleb go, and began mumbling. "He can't talk, but I can't control myself. Which of us is the fool, then? Me, of course. Always me. Isn't that right, soldier?"

"I wouldn't know, sir."

"Yes, you do know, my good fellow. We are all in this together here, and all of us know about each other. But as you were. It is this boy I must apologize to now. Sorry, son, sorry. My fault. I used to get mellow when I was in my cups. But now, I suppose it works the other

171

way. Well, how many bodies this time? Can you count them out for me on your fingers?''

Caleb did so.

"Oh, well," said the doctor, "not as many as yesterday. That's good, I suppose, the poor devils. Yet perhaps they'd all be better off if Major Watts had his way with them more quickly. Don't know why I keep coming here, except I'd probably be shot for desertion. But then again, what would be the harm in that? If you could talk, maybe you would tell me what good I am anyway—a doctor who cannot prescribe medicine because there's none to give! And if there were, what good would it do in this pest hole? Did you see what water these men are drinking from, washing in, and doing everything else?''

Caleb nodded.

"Well, then, at least let me be your doctor. Come to my quarters. I don't use it anymore except to make sure the bourbon in my brain doesn't wear off. And I'd advise you to take a very, very long drink. You shake your head. But you don't understand, my boy. You'll need it to keep away whatever it is that flies through the air from their mouths or brushes off on you at the touch of them. Whatever it is that brings disease and death. Oh yes, it is something that we do not know of and cannot see, but it is there all the same! So I'll ask you again. Will you have a drink with me before we go back out among the tags?''

Again Caleb shook his head. The captain tapped his shoulder. "Quite right. Quite right. No one can drink the war away. That's the true disease. Well, then, are you ready to show me the ones I have to check?''

Caleb nodded, and they went into the field, going slowly from one to another as the doctor felt each tagged

172

pulse for signs of life. As Caleb stood by, waiting to lead him to the next body, he would try to let his imagination carry him away from this place. The scorching sun brought back memories of Grandpa's woolen socks getting singed while the old man warmed his feet at the stove in all weathers. It was harder, though, to pretend being somewhere else while they were moving on among the prisoners, and everywhere there were burning eyes looking up at him from the ground.

A hand tugged at a leg of his pants. "Deadfinder, leave me my tag now," murmured the man whose bony fingers held him. "My angel mother is waiting for me in heaven. Tomorrow I will be with her."

Choking back a sob, Caleb turned to the doctor, who shook his head and said to the prisoner, "Oh, you'll be all right, soldier. Just try to hold on."

"Don't want to anymore," Caleb heard the man say as they walked off.

Slowly they worked their way to the filthy stream, then across it. He made sure to lead the doctor toward the spot where his brother's little rag hung from its sticks. Jonathan, with his head under it, lay clutching something to his ear. The boy slowed as he drew near, turning his head to his brother ever so slightly. Their eyes brushed, and a gaze of wonderment came over Jonathan's. Caleb was passing by when they seemed to light up.

Later that afternoon when he came out leading the grave diggers with their wheelbarrows, Caleb was careful not to go near Jonathan, but he had already begun to form a plan. In the evening he went to town with a note that one of the camp lieutenants wanted him to slip under a young lady's door. After delivering it, he hung around, as if looking at the sights, until it was quite dark. Then he crossed the tracks unseen to knock on the minister's door.

When the kindly old man opened it, Caleb said, ''Reverend, I *can* talk. I'm a Union soldier. My brother is close to dying inside the stockade. I came down south to get him out so he can follow the Drinking Gourd. I don't know as how I've been believing in the goodness of God lately. But if you can help me, I'll be thanking you both every day of my life.''

The old man glanced around in every direction before letting him in.

14

The next morning, just after wake-up, there was a big commotion at the main gate. Guards peered down from the walls while those below who weren't yet on duty hurried to see what was going on. Caleb went with them.

The major stood just outside, screaming at sentries for having dared—having had the downright idiocy—to open the prison gate to a gathering of ladies in their best bonnets and Sunday go-to-meeting clothes. They had baskets of food on their arms and servants trailing them carrying heavier baskets. Parked behind them all were four big wagons in a line, each one loaded down with fresh-picked corn, bushels of peas, tomatoes, cabbages . . . all sorts of good healing food donated by the nearby farms.

"Really, Major," said one of these ladies. "We are not an invasion by the enemy. We are just doing what is right."

The major turned his fury on them. "I cannot permit this!" he cried, waving his arms in the air. "Regulations do not allow it."

"Sir, we do not understand this," the lady replied in a reasonable voice. "Surely these prisoners are no longer a threat to the Confederacy. And Yankee or not, they are human beings. Surely, even you must be touched by pity. And if you do not have enough food to keep them alive, well then, it is our Christian duty to do something about it.''

"You do not know what you are asking!" bellowed the major. "You are giving aid and comfort to the enemy. You are all doing the work of *traitors!*"

"Calm yourself, please, sir. You have seen each of us in town many times over these years. You must be well aware that there's not one of us who doesn't have a son or a husband in the war. Someone in my own case who is never coming back.''

"I cannot argue with you. You have no right to be here. Go away. I demand you go away!"

A carriage had been driving up. Caleb now watched the doctor getting out. He came up through the crowd on unsteady legs. "Excuse me, ladies," he murmured, touching the brim of his hat. "I have to go inside."

"Doctor, you must tell this man to stop being so inhuman.''

"He is a major, madam. He is allowed to be more inhuman than only a captain like myself. Please allow me to pass.''

"What? You make a *joke* of this? Are you or are you not a man of medicine? And before you became a soldier, did you not take an oath to heal the sick?"

"I will not discuss this with you, madam," he said, flushing.

"No, I can see you are too drunk to discuss anything."

"Blessedly so, madam."

He tipped his hat, passing through, but his face had turned beet-red. Seeing Caleb among the onlookers, he grabbed him tightly by the arm. "Let's get started. I don't want to just stand here!"

In the field once more, they worked together finding and tagging. "What did those women expect of me?" the captain muttered to himself, feeling the wrist of a dead man. "Orders are orders. How can I go against my commanding officer, no matter what kind of monster he is?"

Baines was still talking to himself more than an hour later when they crossed the foul stream. From here on, Caleb began looking for a chance to get to his brother unnoticed. It came when the doctor bent over a body not fifteen feet from Jonathan. Drifting away quickly, Caleb knelt beside him, reaching out with the tag.

"Get that away from me, Deadfinder!" gasped a fright-filled voice. "I'm alive!"

Bony, but amazingly strong, hands closed over the boy's own arm. Long fingernails dug into his flesh. Other prisoners were near enough to stir where they lay and cock their heads.

"I'm Caleb!" the boy breathed into the face of the wild-eyed man. "Don't you remember? You recognized me this morning! You've got to let go. Play dead, or we're lost!"

He had counted on the drunkenness of the captain to keep him from being sharp-eyed. But Baines, getting up from the last man, started to lumber toward him. Instantly Caleb was on his feet pointing to a body farther on.

"Wait, I haven't examined this one yet. And you gave him a tag."

Jonathan's eyes were still and staring when the doctor bent over to lift his arm and take his pulse. Caleb watched

Baines's fingers slide down to the wrist. Everything depended on this moment. Everything!

"But *this* man isn't . . ."

"He's my brother!" Caleb frantically hissed in the medical officer's ear, dropping beside him. "Please don't take the tag off!"

The doctor's mouth opened and closed before he spoke. Even then it was in a tone of wonderment. "You're a Yankee spy . . ."

"What's there to spy on *here?* Is this what will win or lose the war? I got into this place to bring my brother home!"

"Do you really think," muttered the captain between his gritted teeth, "that I give a fig or a feather about your brother or anyone else's?"

"Yes!" whispered Caleb fiercely. "I think it—and I know it!"

The captain's thumb was still on the beating pulse, but the hand trembled, and he gazed into nothingness. "This would be aiding the enemy . . ."

"Does my brother look like he'll be carrying a gun?"

Dr. Baines glanced up at the high wall, then down at Jonathan, whose eyes now darted back and forth between them. "Even if you get him out of here, he'll smother before you can dig him out of the pit."

"Help me, anyway."

In hope, fear, and prayer the brothers gazed at him.

The captain stood up. "Where is that next body?" he said shakily.

Trembling himself, Caleb led him away.

15

<hr>

When it rained hard in the afternoon, Caleb grew afraid the grave diggers wouldn't be coming. But they pushed their wheelbarrows through the main gate with their slave driver behind them, leaving their wagons outside waiting for bodies.

Caleb looked at each in turn, and one of them—a strong man black as midnight—blinked three times. This was Martin. Caleb led them into the stockade, pointing out one body after another. He saved Jonathan for last. Martin lifted the "body" gently, setting him down on another one—and wheeled him from the muddy field.

Caleb went out through the main gate to watch how his brother was stacked among the corpses. It was at the top. When the wagons drove away to the burial ground, he followed on foot and stopped beside the slave driver at the side of the road while the wheelbarrows were being taken down.

As they looked on together, the slave driver gave him a playful nudge with his elbow. "Now, that's whut I like to see—a feller who takes a real interest in how his work turns out."

With a shrug and a grin Caleb reached down under his tucked-in shirt and drew out a bottle of corn mash whiskey. He pulled the stopper and offered the first drink to the slave master.

"Now, that's right thoughtful. Don't mind if I do."

Caleb watched him tilt the bottle up. So did Martin, who quickly wheeled Jonathan out of sight behind a mound.

Other slaves had noticed. Confused and fearful, they stopped pushing their wheelbarrows. The slave driver, finishing his pull at the bottle, was just about to look up. Caleb made a quick gesture to take another swig.

"Why thank ye, kindly. Do believe I will."

With an angry wave, meanwhile, Martin got the men to go back to working.

The slave driver, who expected Caleb to drink with him, watched his Adam's apple rise and fall while he swallowed. They passed the bottle back and forth until it was empty. By then the pit had been completely covered over . . . or so it appeared. When the wheelbarrows and the slaves were all back on the wagons, he gave the sweating boy a parting clap on the back. Caleb threw up as soon as they were gone. Still that didn't clear his reeling head. He needed to get to that mound and start tearing away at that layer of dirt! His legs gave way under him as he staggered towards it . . . and he fell.

It was the minister who later brought him to his feet and led him to a buckboard. Jonathan was already in it, lying under a horse blanket. A mare that seemed as old as its owner drove off with them—but not toward the town.

The road they turned onto was little more than a path. They had to make stops to rest the horse and feed it handfuls of hay. Once they pulled into a grove of trees just before a couple of hard riding men on horseback galloped by.

Strange to say, the brothers did not talk. It was as if they had nothing to tell each other. Nothing at least that could yet be put into words. But Caleb held Jonathan's hand, feeling like a little boy again whose big brother was taking him for a walk. And when Jonathan fell asleep in the middle of eating a crust of bread, Caleb stroked his hair.

He had been thinking meanwhile of what to say to this wonderful man who was risking so much to help strangers. But when he tried to put his thankfulness into words, he began to sob instead. The minister gently pressed his shoulder. "That's it, son. That's the way. Those tears are as good as a prayer—and the Lord hears it. Yes, he has heard many a healing prayer just like that one."

It was a white family of Quaker farmers who took the Peasley brothers next. The minister drove back to town, leaving them hidden in a secret room built into a hayloft that had long been a "station" on the Underground Railroad.

Jonathan, the family thought, was unfit to travel. Nor did they dare feed him very much during those first few days. He was started, almost like a baby, on food that was easy to digest, watery vegetable soup, thin porridge, and teas made from tree bark, roots, and herbs. Later there was boiled chicken with broth. As he grew a bit stronger they happily served huckleberry jam with his thick porridge, corn bread, and eggs with bacon, mashed potatoes with pork, apple Betty with cream, and hominy grits. They read to the boys from the bible and watched out down the road when Jonathan was able to begin short walks in the woods.

On market day the farmer's wife took a buckboard into Sanderson—a two-hour ride each way—to get the news. She came back with word that there was no news. The plot had not been discovered. And as for a young soldier who had gone missing, "why there was something wrong with him, anyway," so it was said—and no search was going on.

There was heavy fighting again up above Richmond. The armies, like two boxers, were ducking in different directions to outsmart each other. It would be very dangerous, she told her husband, to try using their old contacts to smuggle these two north to the Union lines.

"But keeping them here much longer," he replied in a troubled tone, "is dangerous, too."

This was when Caleb asked a question that had already been on his mind. "How far are we from the ocean?"

After waiting a few days longer for Jonathan to gain strength, the brothers set out on a big hike going east. In their wide black hats and long black clothes they were a sight that people along the way found strange. Yes, but not too strange, since folks knew about Quakers, and some had even seen a few before. What's more, Caleb had an idea by now how to sound "southern."

As for the brothers, they didn't mind the long cross-country walk. Heck, a hundred miles or so was nothing a couple of foot soldiers of the Twentieth Maine hadn't done before, even if it had been at different times. There was food tightly packed in their little bags and much to talk about on the open road or while crossing a field with no one to overhear.

It was while they were standing in a stream, looking for fish to spear with pointed sticks, that Caleb told his brother how Abby had heard him being described as a traitor and a deserter. Jonathan was less upset than he expected. "If she loves me, she won't believe it," he said simply. Then he told what had actually happened.

"We'd captured the town the day before. But that was easy enough because the enemy was dug in above us on the heights. Well, we needed to travel light, so we were ordered to unsling our knapsacks and blankets before we moved out to join the attack on that hill. The regiments charging up it ahead of us had been mowed down by the worst cross fire I'd ever seen. Now it was our turn be cut to ribbons. We were stopped in our tracks, and we threw ourselves to the ground, taking cover any way we could." Jonathan broke off quickly. "Caleb, there's a trout right there."

"Where?"

"Right under you . . . No, not there, between your legs . . . You missed it!"

"All right, so I missed it. That's not the end of the world."

"Did I say it was?"

"Just go on with your story of woe," grumbled Caleb, cross with himself and taking it out on his brother.

"Well, we were pinned down on that slope for hours— and when the battle sweat dried off us, we began to shiver. That was when I learned that even in the south a winter night can be bitter cold. At least, though, I had my coat, but some of the men had left theirs behind, along with their packs. Rather than freeze to death, they started stripping the corpses. I'd been dozing when I felt mine being unbuttoned. The fellow had taken me for dead, I suppose—you know how quietly I sleep. But when I suddenly shoved him off me, thinking that would be enough, he hit me hard with his fist and my head fell back against a rock.''

"He must have been crazy," said Caleb.

"Maybe I was, too, for not saying something before I started wrestling with him. Anyway, I went out like a light, and by the time I came to again, there was a rebel's bayonet against my throat. How many hours had gone by, I don't know. I'd been half stripped, the battle was over, and our army was gone. Some prisoners were being shot, I think. But I was lucky, if you call it that. I landed in Sanderson.''

Another wriggling fish swam by, but neither of them now was set for it. "One of our own did that to you?"

"Caleb, there are all kinds on all sides. Don't you know that by now?"

"Guess I do. But making slaves of other people is wrong.''

"That it is—though not everybody on our side knows it. Hey, what do you say we get back to the business of catching ourselves a fine dinner?"

Caleb brightened, and not long afterwards they did indeed have a fine campfire meal. They slept in a pine grove on beds of ground cover as soft as feathers. They talked about home and told stories about Grandpa that made them giggle like children.

They got up with the sun, and there were times while they were pushing on that this "escape" almost began to feel like a holiday! It wasn't until the rainy night they drew near to the ocean that they sensed danger.

Caleb still had the guard's blade with him. And Jonathan, scarecrow that he was, still had his long, powerful hands.

The street sloped down to the harbor of the little village. When he saw the softly rippling tide water rolling in and out, Caleb felt as if his chest would explode. He glanced at his brother. Jonathan's eyes were glittering.

Down on the shore they found a little skiff tied to a dock. She looked shipshape and, though she was empty, smelled heavily of fish. It was perfect, but Jonathan held back, and finally he shook his head. Caleb understood without a word being said. This would be stealing from a fisherman just like themselves.

Trotting along the water's edge, they came to a small boat that had been damaged and pulled up on the beach. Caleb was reminded of the *Dolphin;* this craft had a bent mast.

"I think we can get that jib up at least," Jonathan said. "Might be enough to get us away from here if the wind keeps up from the west. Then we'll have to paddle some and hope we get picked up by one of our own."

They hauled it out of the water, got in, Caleb pushing off with a pole. The tiny triangle of a sail in front of the leaning mast caught enough breeze to move them along about as far as the mouth of the bay. But then the wind shifted and died off.

They were in danger of drifting back!

"Here!" Caleb tossed his brother the end a length of rope. "You lash this as high as you can up the mast, and I'll pull back and brace it to the cleat by the rudder. We'll get that mainsail up!"

"First heavy wind off the beam, she'll crack and go over on the lee side."

"She won't if I wrap myself around her and hold on."

"You're that strong are you, my little pup of a brother?"

"When I have to be."

"Don't I know it! But let's see what else we can wrap around her as well."

It was an hour's work before they were really under way. Jonathan watched him taking deep gulps of salt air as they left the inlet for open water. "You look happy out here," he said. "Like you were made for the sea."

"Aren't you?"

"Oh, I'm like Pa. We know it well enough, but there are times when we think it a lonely place. But you, Caleb—Grandpa is convinced the wandering Peasley soul skipped over us and into you."

"But *you* wandered."

"No, I joined; and only because of the . . ." All at once, Jonathan fell silent.

"What is it?"

"I smell something."

Caleb sniffed the air . . . and he, too, caught a faint trace of smoke.

"There's a steamer somewhere out there," declared his brother, pointing into the darkness off the starboard side.

"Why don't we hear the engines then?"

"Maybe she's laying low."

"There's only one reason to be doing that!" declared Caleb, suddenly shifting sail.

The dark shape ahead proved he'd guessed right about what the vessel was doing there. She was a U.S. Navy cutter, her flag flying high, her guns aimed low. It was on rainy nights such as this when Confederate smugglers and raiders would try to slip through the great Union blockade. Her engines were banked almost to the point of shutting off, but they were still letting out a little steam. The fighting ship was keeping herself ready to spring like a cat.

Small as their little skiff was, Caleb decided not to take chances on being mistaken for an enemy. A smart captain, he thought, remembering the *Dolphin*'s encounter with a sinking raider, would be wary of some sort of a trick . . . a boat rigged to explode perhaps. He ran down the sail to let the skiff float while those on board the cutter had a chance to study them.

But it was Caleb whom Jonathan had been studying. "I want you to know," he now began, "how very grateful I—"

"Some other time," the embarrassed boy said quickly.

"Why do you keep cutting me off!"

"Look."

A dory was being lowered from the cutter. Three men climbed down to it on a rope ladder. Caleb thought the man with a pistol in his hand was probably the ship's first mate. The two seamen rowing had muskets at the ready across their laps. As soon as they pulled alongside, the mate asked questions while his men boarded the skiff, searching them first, then the boat. When the mate felt satisfied that all was well, he took the brothers into his boat, leaving the skiff adrift.

The cutter, they learned over piping hot cups of cocoa in the chart room, was almost at the end of her tour of duty and would soon be bound for refueling at the great naval station up in Annapolis, Maryland. From there, they could send the good news flying ahead by telegram to Abby and the family while they set out for Maine.

"Right here and now," declared Jonathan firmly as the pair stepped out on the deck, "is that *other time* you keep putting me off to. I just want to say there isn't anyone I can think of who'd do what you did for a brother."

Caleb looked up at the clearing sky. "Well, I can think of someone."

"Who?"

"You."

Caleb felt his arm being taken hold of. He smiled and, looking up at the stars, sought out the Big Dipper. "They call it *following the Drinking Gourd,*" he said.

"Who do?"

"People running away from slavery to freedom."

The hand on his arm tightened. "Home," Jonathan murmured, putting so much meaning into that one word that it vibrated in the air like the buzzing of a hive.

"Home," Caleb repeated, tracing a line to the North Star.